Christmas in Dancing Deer

Christmas in Dancing Deer

Celebrating the Holidays in Small-Town America

**Continuing the Award Winning Dancing Deer Series
with Book Five**

Ron Lambert

Published in the United States by:

Printers Guild Publishing House

425 Spring Street, Suite 101
Columbus, Texas 78934-2461
(979) 732-2963
Fax (979) 733-0015
www.printersguildpublishing.com

Library of Congress Control Number: 2013904460

ISBN 978-0-9855083-3-3

Trademarks

Christmas in Dancing Deer is a work of Fiction

Except for some historical personages, the names, characters, and incidents of the story are used fictitiously and do not represent any actual person or event.

Some of the towns, cities, or geographic localities are real. An interested reader might be able to find Lee Mountain, the Buffalo River, the Illinois Bayou, the Big Piney, Moccasin Gap, or even Little Creek's water crossing. Eudy's Drug and Fountain might be harder.

The author grew up in a small, rural community and saw wonder in all living things. He wrote this story using the hazy remembrances of a child's fertile imagination and sheer luck.

Cover

Art from Dreamstime.com

Table of Contents

CAST OF CHARACTERS

City Mayor

Robert Springer (Mayor Bob the Bull) and wife, Clarice

Members of City Council

Rube Abernathy and wife, Suzanne
Johnston Baker and wife, Betty
Harold Greenleaf and wife, Imogene
Jerry Millhouse and wife, Mona
Paul Nelson
Faisal Obadiah and wife, Ophelia
Bill Potter and wife, Harriet
George Satterfield and wife, Summer
Edwin Stanky and wife, Gladys
Stone and wife, Marge
Boyd and girlfriend, Stacy Jo Martin

Orphans

Spencer and sister, Millie
Terrell and sister, Penny
Andy, Judd, Lacy, Lawrence, Tyrone
Frieda, Laurie, Miranda, Monica, Sherry, Teresa

Employees at the *Gilded Lily*

Madam -- Betts
Prostitutes – Cassie, Jennifer, Linda, Marianne, Naomi, Rosalinda, Saucy, Twinkie, Miss Ryan

CHAPTER 1 – ST. BARTHOLOMEW'S ORPHANAGE

Monday afternoon, December 3, 1945

With a heavy heart, Father Donovan O'Reilly descended the steps of the bus to the pavement. For the past fifteen years, he had been one of the three priests officiating at St. Bartholomew's Holy Catholic Church. Besides his occasional homily on Sunday morning he officially was in charge of the seven boys and ten girls residing in northern Arkansas' largest orphanage.

During the depression, desperate people brought their children to the church saying they couldn't feed them. With tears in their eyes, they handed over malnourished waifs, promising to come back if they found work. When Franklin Delano Roosevelt became president, replacing an ineffective Herbert Hoover, he immediately set the wheels in motion to get Americans back on the job. If business didn't want America's unemployed, the government did. Millions of men went to work for Uncle Sam building public works projects. Then the war knocked on America's door and jobs became plentiful. With people getting regular paychecks, the torrent of children being admitted to St. Bartholomew's diminished, with more leaving than arriving. Those mothers and fathers looking for better times were now prosperous enough to take care of their own and came running for their children. Additionally, some of the boys and girls had reached the age to enter the workforce and left with the blessing of the church. And poor families who wanted children but couldn't have them, now found they could afford to adopt.

Father O'Reilly thought back a few years to when there were forty or more children under his guidance with only fifteen or so available for adoption. Now all seventeen were available. And soon, if the church hierarchy has its way, there will be no children at all in the sacred confines of St. Bartholomew's.

"Good afternoon, Father. I hope you had a pleasant trip."

"Good afternoon, Jesse. Does the paper always greet arriving passengers?"

Jesse Bell was the owner and editor of the *Marsden County Meteor*, a semi-weekly newspaper distributed every Wednesday and Saturday morning. "No, I was just passing by. I've been to Ridley Field to see how the workers are coming on our new ballpark. It looks like they'll finish in a couple of months. You got any news you can give me?"

"Not right now. It was just a regular ecclesiastical meeting to see how we can cut costs while still helping those who seek, find the road to salvation."

"Then they're going to keep the orphanage open?"

"Jesse, are you privy to information not available to the general public?"

"No, Father. I just keep up with current events and have a knack for putting two and two together."

The town vagrant walked up wearing a stretched sock over an abundance of unruly hair. "Father, would you like me to take your luggage to the rectory?"

"No, Cody. I've only got the one piece. I'll carry it myself. Thank you for offering though." Father Donovan O'Reilly took a step to retrieve his luggage, stopped, and turned to face Jesse Bell. "Jesse, give me a little time to break the news to the children."

"No problem. Will you sit down with me so I can write an in-depth article?"

"Sure. How about Wednesday afternoon? Give me a chance to get my wind back."

"Certainly. I'll bring a photographer for taking pictures of the kids at their desks or, maybe, of you lecturing to them. I'll also bring my assistant to accurately write down the particulars of our interview."

"Jesse, be careful what you say to the children. I don't imagine they will be in the best of spirits." With that, Father O'Reilly walked to his luggage. Now how did Jesse figure out the church was going to close the orphanage? Who else knows?

It was three blocks from the bus station to the church. Along the way, the priest was greeted by several people. Everyone wanted to stop and talk. They asked about his health and told him about theirs. They asked where he'd traveled and if he had found the bus comfortable, if he'd encountered any bad weather, if he'd read any good books, if he'd heard that former chief of police, W.W. Wainwright, had been found and had returned to Dancing Deer the week before. Several people offered to carry his suitcase.

A few hours later, he dropped in on the children's evening meal. Lacy had just finished blessing the food and all seventeen were greedily filling their plates from bowls strategically placed in the middle of a long table. Instead of the children separating according to gender, the boys and girls mixed, with the youngest off to one side. The older children, now old enough to consider themselves grown up, had taken the remainder of the table. They liked to talk about more important matters than what the younger children discussed at the far end.

When Father O'Reilly walked in, everyone looked his way and stopped eating. The priest was not known for socializing and, if he came during one of their meals, he had something to say.

"I hope everyone had a nice vacation while I was gone."

Tyrone said, "Father, it's no vacation for us when you're not here. Sister Mary and Sister Margaret have given us enough assignments that, after we finish supper, we have to go work on them."

"Not me," said a little red-headed girl. "I don't like doing math. Who cares when those two trains collide? I want to learn to sew."

"Well now, Penny, you have to learn it all. You're too young to pick and choose. That'll come later—after you've mastered a little bit of all the disciplines: a little history, a little math, some biology, grammar and penmanship, and English literature. By the way, has anyone finished reading *The Count of Monte Cristo*?"

All hands from the older group went up.

"How about *Pride and Prejudice*?"

All the girl's hands went up.

"*Tom Sawyer*?"

All the boy's hands went up.

"That's about as I expected." Father Donovan O'Reilly sat in a chair a few feet from the table. "You may continue eating while we talk." He waited a moment before proceeding. "Has anyone been to St. Louis or New Orleans?"

Teresa raised her hand. "I've been to New Orleans. My mother bought me a pastry, coated with powdered sugar. I ate it while standing on the waterfront. There were ships moving in the water in front of me, and the top of the water was higher than my head. It was creepy."

"Teresa, you might get an opportunity to see New Orleans again." Father O'Reilly looked around the room. No one was eating. They looked at him, waiting for an explanation. "A few years ago, every Catholic church had lots of children just like yourselves waiting for a new family. But now a lot of our churches have no children and others have only a handful. At St. Bartholomew's we have seventeen and that's the most of any church in northern Arkansas. But the church thinks it would be better for you if it consolidated by having its churches send their children to places where it could accommodate a larger number. As soon as the church gets it worked out, some of you will relocate to St. Louis with others going to New Orleans or Chicago. There you'll get better instruction. It'll be just like regular school. There will be separate teachers for each field of study and each teacher will be better qualified to teach his subject. Here the two sisters and I teach everything. I might do well in math, but I'm not that competent in biology or English grammar. Neither of the two sisters likes government and neither knows how to sew. Penny, in the public schools they call that home economics. And besides sewing you'll learn to cook—which is another thing the two sisters don't do very well."

Terrell raised his hand, "We can't go together to the new place?"

"I doubt it Terrell. They haven't got the specifics figured out yet, but it looks like the girls will go one place and the boys another, with those five and younger going to a third location. I'll accompany each group, returning here between trips."

"That stinks. Did they think about asking us first?"

"No. I don't think anyone thought to ask for your opinion. It's a pity. You might have come up with a better solution."

A little blond-haired girl started crying. "I don't want to go somewhere else. I like it here."

"Me too."

"Separate places for the boys and girls and young ones means breaking up brothers and sisters. Did you tell them that?"

"Spencer, I'm sorry to say that I didn't say anything to anybody. I was the youngest one there and spent most of my time listening to grumbling old men. They had already made up their minds. But here's what we can do. I want everyone to work together making a list of grievances you have with their proposed plan. Come up with your own solution. Don't necessarily think of what's best for you, but what's best for the church, and something you can live with. I'll present it, I promise." Father O'Reilly looked around the room locking eyes with each of his charges. He then nodded and said, "We've got a month. Nothing's supposed to happen until after the holidays."

CHAPTER 2 – MERLE

Tuesday morning, December 4, 1945

"Merle, I don't want to."

"Now, you listen to me. You go into the bank and hand the woman behind that wire cage this note. She's got our money. She'll put all our money in a sack and give it to you. Look real mean. Make a frown like you shouldn't have to ask for it, cause it's ours." Merle waited. "Lenny, make a frown." A pause. "Come on, you can do better than that. Give a low snarl."

"Grrr rr."

"That's it. Talk real low so only the teller can hear. Now keep your hand in your pocket like you're holding a gun."

"Merle, what if she don't like me? What am I gonna do if she don't give me our money?"

"Then you come outside and tell me. I'll park the car and get it myself. When you come out hold the sack in front so I can see it. Lenny, don't run. Okay, you got it?"

"Merle, I don't want to. You do it and I'll do anything else you want. You want me to knock down a man so you can grab his money, yank away a woman's purse, chase down a boy on a bicycle. I'll do it, Merle, but don't make me go in there by myself."

"What you scared of, Lenny? I'll be right here. Ain't I always looked out for you? Ain't I always taken care of you? Shared my food with you?"

"Yeah, I guess so."

"Okay, then. Here's the note. Stand in line, and when its your turn you give it to the lady. If she don't give you our money, you come tell me."

Tears started welling up in Lenny's eyes. He knew she wasn't going to give him their money, and Merle would be mad and hit him. Lenny raised his cuff to wipe away tears trickling down both sides of his nose. He sniffled, took the note, and opened the car door. Then he waited a moment, hoping Merle would change his mind.

"Go on, big guy. We'll take our money and head west. You always said you wanted to see a cowboy."

Merle thought Lenny had a good chance of getting the money. He was a big guy, rough looking, dirty clothes. As soon as he handed the lady the note she would shake in her boots. Not give him the money? Hell, nowadays those tellers say life's too short to take a chance. It's not their money. Give up the money and live another day. Lenny would soon be strolling out that door with a sack full of money and they'd be good for a month or two. Merle thought he'd better roll down the window and make sure the door was unlocked.

Just then the front door of the bank flew open and Lenny charged out. He held the sack in both hands as he ran to the car.

"Stop. Hold it right there. Put your hands in the air."

"Lenny, throw in the sack."

There was an explosion. Blood started spewing from Lenny's chest. He fell against the car. A few bills from the top of the sack fell through the window opening. "Merle, don't leave me. I got our money." Lenny slumped as his legs gave way. Sliding down the side of the car he desperately grabbed at the door handle.

Merle locked the door and stepped on the accelerator.

"Merle? Please, Merle? Don't leave me."

CHAPTER 3 – HIDING

Wednesday morning, December 5, 1945

That damn Lenny. Got the money then ran for the door. Probably knocked someone down on the way, drawing the attention of the security guard. Serves him right, getting shot like that. No way I can be linked. Lenny didn't know my real name, the car's license plate's been removed, no papers of any kind, and no one getting close enough to the car to get a good look at me. All anyone could see was a black Ford and there's thousands of them.

Merle checked into the Ritz Grand Hotel with a small suitcase. He'd been hidden for an entire day while the police searched the highways. Now it was time to make another score; then head to California. The town looked prosperous enough: shiny new bank, lots of retail stores with Christmas merchandise, shoppers everywhere wearing heavy coats and carrying packages. He'd scope out the town, find an easy target or two, grab their money, and head west.

After depositing a suitcase in his room, Merle went to the restaurant. Nine fifty-dollar bills had fallen through the window when that copper shot Lenny. Providence was giving him a break to make up for all his previous efforts that had gone awry. Well, not every job was a bust. There was that Western Union office. He and Lenny had managed to walk out of there with three thousand. Merle wondered how much had been in Lenny's sack.

At the restaurant's check-out counter sat a stack of newspapers. Merle put a dime in a saucer and took out fifty cents. He also took the top copy. A waitress led him to an empty table while Merle casually glanced over the front page. "Bank Heist Foiled" was emblazoned across the top in inch-high letters. Merle sat down and ordered coffee.

Damn, Lenny didn't die—not yet. He's in intensive care here in Dancing Deer's general hospital. Well, I'll be.

"No. I haven't had a chance to look yet. But bring me a short stack and three strips of bacon. You got maple syrup?"

Merle read the article, the letters to the editor, an article about a new ballpark being built, sales going on at the stores, a food pantry giving out free food, and the church section offering anyone needing a place to stay the night a warm bed. It looked like each church was trying to outdo its competition. Merle decided to check out the bank and those churches. They probably had a small amount of cash stashed away in case a family needed assistance. Easy pickings.

Merle left the Ritz Bistro and walked down Main Street until he came to the First Bank and Trust of Dancing Deer. He walked inside. Huge vault with massive door. Must have lots of money. One security guard—no, two security guards. The second walked out of the vault with a briefcase chained to his wrist. He and a man in a suit left the bank. Merle followed at a distance.

"These first few times I'll go with you. We need to get the procedure down and let the depositors know that when they give their money to us it's the same as delivering it in person to the bank."

"Mr. Jimmerson, how you gonna know how much each one deposits?"

"It'll be just like at the bank, Mr. Stanky. They make out a deposit slip, listing each check and the total amount of cash. I verify the amounts listed and their math, give them a receipt, and stuff the envelope holding their money through the slot in the top of your traveling bank vault. Then we bid *adieu* and head to our next store. If we get the satchel full we have to go back to the bank where the cashier uses her key to remove it from your wrist, straps on another, and off we go. I think Mr. Potter's idea was wonderful. After we've got it operating smoothly, I'll turn over my job to another bank employee."

"I can sure use the extra work. I've got my eye on a pearl necklace and matching earrings for Gladys' Christmas present."

"Are you going to be able to do this every morning and still get your shift done for Chief Trent."

"Oh, sure. The morning shift is the one everyone covets. I asked to trade for the one in the afternoon through Christmas and had two offers. But I have to be done here and at headquarters by three every day."

"That should be no problem. Okay, here we are at our first depositor."

CHAPTER 4 – A NEW PLAN
Wednesday morning, December 5, 1945

"I think they ought to give us a list of the orphanages they're going to keep open and let us choose which one."

"Yeah, and pictures showing us where we'd sleep and eat and . . . and . . ."

"And play. We need to know if they've got playground equipment, a ball field, and if they've got a creek or a pond close by."

"How many books in their library."

"And what the sisters look like. I think I can spot the nasty ones."

"You didn't spot Sister Margaret."

"Yeah, I know. But I'm better now. I can recognize those that don't like kids by their squinty little eyes and smirk. You wait. I've got it figured out."

"Terrell, you got the blank paper?"

"Yep."

"I think we ought to get a list of the possible choices from Father O'Reilly. The one in Chicago is going to have cold winters. I've read that arctic blasts coming down from the north pole are bone chilling, the winter waters in Newfoundland Bay will send a person into cardiac arrest in ninety seconds, but the wind blowing through Chicago from Lake Michigan is even worse and will numb your senses. You die standing up or leaning against a lamp pole without even knowing what's happening."

"And the one in New Orleans will have mosquitoes the size of hummingbirds. We'll go to sleep at night and wake up in the morning covered with red welts and not left with enough blood to excite a vampire."

"Spencer, I want to go with you. When Mom left, you said you'd take care of me. How you gonna do that if they send us to different cities? We've always been together."

"I know, Millie. We'll think of something. Maybe that family you went to visit last spring will send a request for another interview."

"Naw, I don't want to live there. They only wanted someone to take care of their baby. I would've spent my days and nights changing diapers."

"Listen, you two. We got a problem to solve. Let's tackle it first."

"Okay, but I think Lawrence was right about getting a list of the places where we could go. What if they have a place in Florida—or California?"

"I choose Oregon. I saw a *National Geographic* one time that had pictures of the biggest trees you ever saw. Everything was lush and green. I'd like to live there."

"There are no trees bigger than the giant Sequoias in northern California."

"Father O'Reilly said someone from the paper was coming this afternoon to take pictures. Maybe we can have it put in the paper how the church never asked us what we wanted. I don't think they'd want bad publicity."

"Hey, maybe that's it. We'll have a pity party. Let the town think they've let us down. And now the church is herding us off to God-knows-where before the people in Dancing Deer can make it right. We could talk about how the other kids in town won't play with us; how the stores ask to see our money before they show us anything from their counters; or how the people at City Park make us bathe before we get in the swimming pool when they don't ask anyone else to do the same."

"That's not true."

"Maybe not in general, but it could be true on occasion. Newspapers need news—and conflict. That's what sells papers."

CHAPTER 5 – JESSE

Wednesday afternoon, December 5, 1945

"Father, what can you tell me and, of that, what will you allow me to print in the paper?"

"The Lord's house doesn't keep secrets. You may print anything you think is true. But would you mind showing me the article before you go to press? I need to show it to my superiors. They don't like surprises."

"Fair enough."

"I've told the children and they're coming up with their own solution. I promised I'd present any alternative plan they thought would satisfy the church and they could live with. This morning I gave them a list of the locations the church is thinking about moving them to. They are adamant against breaking up brothers and sisters."

"I don't blame them. Father, the church wouldn't intentionally do that, would it?"

"The church doesn't look at it the same way as the children. The little ones think their older siblings are their safety-nets—the last vestige of what had once been a happy life. The church thinks it now provides that role and makes its decisions based on what is most efficient and, therefore, what is most economical."

"Did you tell the church council not to break up brother from sister?"

"No. They'd already made up their minds and I was too slow to speak out. Now that I've thought about it, I think the children are right and I plan on helping them with their plan. And when it's completed, I'll be presenting it to the men making the final decision. In the meantime, it's Christmas. Although I don't want to give them any false hope, I do want to raise their spirits."

"What can the paper do? Father, how can the readers of my paper help?"

"Love these children like I do. They're good boys and girls, never doing anything wrong, or getting into trouble. I think they will all turnout to be fine upstanding citizens. Maybe you could write a paragraph about each one, because, if one got adopted it would cause a campus-wide celebration."

"I think I will. I'll devote half the paper to the children and have every member of my staff contribute articles. Would you make the children available?"

"Certainly."

"Good. Let's go to the classrooms and get some pictures."

In the first classroom the priest announced, "Boys, this is Mr. Bell. He's the owner and editor of the *Marsden County Meteor*. He's come to take pictures, to talk to some of you, and to get your views on being relocated to another orphanage. Please give a big round of applause for Mr. Jesse Bell." Father O'Reilly reached over and shook Jesse's hand saying, "I'm getting ready for a stint at Ringling Brothers."

"So the church wants to move you. Anybody here want that to happen? Can I get a show of hands of those in favor of a new place to live?" Jesse looked around the room where no hands were raised. "Okay then, what's your plan to get them to change their mind?"

Terrell slowly raised his hand. "We don't have any specifics yet, just an overall agreement that we want to stay here with Father O'Reilly."

"And the two nuns?"

"No. They can go."

"I see. Is there anything the town can do to help?"

Several hands went up. Lawrence said, "Actually, sir, the town hasn't done anything to help or hinder us. They shun us. The other boys and girls don't play with us. We're not invited to any of their activities and when we invite them to come to ours, they don't show. The town doesn't think we don't exist."

"Is that right? I know you exist."

"Excuse me, Mr. Bell, have you been to one of our plays?"

"Uh . . . no. Have you had one recently?"

"*The passion of Christ, our Savior* last Easter. Four people outside the church were here. We canceled it after the first performance."

"My goodness. Are you planning another for this Christmas?"

"No. And no invitation has been received for any party, any play, any dance, or anything whatsoever that the town's putting on."

"You might be right. Maybe the town doesn't know you exist. Have there been any adoptions by a Dancing Deer family?"

"Not during the last five years."

"Will any of you be going anywhere for the holidays?"

"No, sir. No one has anywhere to go."

"No families at all?"

"Yes, Frieda receives letters from her two older brothers and younger sister. They're with three different families in two different states. She hasn't seen them since she was two. She probably would've been adopted as well had she not had the measles. We stood in a line and had to show the prospective families our teeth and tell them how we came to be in an orphanage in the first place. I don't think any of the families wanted children who came from parents who died of a disease. They wondered if it could be inherited or if we were contagious. It was degrading."

"If that's the case, why do you want to stay in Dancing Deer?"

"This is our home. We've come to accept what little is offered. It's beautiful here. We love the town."

Spencer said, "We read your paper every time it comes out. Do you know who the secret donor is? Terrell thinks it's Mr. Ridley—although, he's now dead. I thought it might be that Frenchman who worked for Mr. Jellico. I've heard he owns most of France. Lacy thinks Mr. Mellon or Mr. Carnegie came through town on a vacation. Do you know?"

"No, I don't. Do you think if you knew who he was, he might help you out of your present situation?"

"We don't want charity. We want an equal opportunity."

"I see. Do you think Father O'Reilly can give you that?"

"Father O'Reilly is the best friend we've got. He looks out for us and doesn't talk down to us. Everyone here is trying to learn something so he will have a skill when old enough to leave. Father O'Reilly tries to help, but there's not many jobs for someone whose best skill is Latin or math. Maybe you could convince the town to conduct learning sessions so we could become welders, auto mechanics, or operate heavy equipment. Anything would help."

"Young man, that's a wonderful idea. I'll start on it this afternoon. Is everyone here in agreement?"

Five young men and two little boys yelled "Yes."

The photographer took pictures and, while doing so, felt the need to explain how a camera worked. And he continued with why the lighting had to be placed so there would not be shadows under noses, chins, or deep-set eyes. The boys followed him around the room and posed when asked. Jesse talked to each boy while Mitzi, his assistant, wrote it down.

An hour later two nuns came in from working with the girls and took over the boys. Father Donovan O'Reilly, the two men, and the young lady from the paper moved in the adjoining classroom with the ten girls.

Later that afternoon Jesse Bell started to write. It would be his most stirring work. He decided not to try to make Saturday's paper. He would need to research each orphan's story and coordinate several related smaller articles. He now planned on devoting almost the entire paper to the plight of the children. And he needed a little extra time to run it by the church's authorities. Jesse smiled. This was going to be his best work and he decided to give himself until the deadline for Wednesday's paper on the nineteenth. He called Genevieve and told her he'd be late getting home. He had so much enthusiasm in his voice she had a hard time believing he was working and not partying. But he was her Jesse and, to her knowledge, he was not interested in parties—just hard work.

CHAPTER 6 – EDWIN

Thursday evening, December 6, 1945

"Edwin, I'd like to buy you something special for Christmas. Can you give me some hints?"

"What's with you, sweetie? You've never bought me anything before. That is . . . except for that first Christmas when you bought me deerskin houseshoes. I got you a puppy. Remember?"

"Yes, I remember. We were so much in love. I believed you were the most wonderful man on earth. Then Ajax chewed up your new slippers. I thought you were going to beat that little dog, but you picked him up, looked him straight in the eye, and said, 'Ajax, I'm the alpha dog around here.' Then you hauled him to the Livery Feed and Seed and bought him some rawhide sticks."

"Yep, them were the softest shoes I ever wore."

Gladys picked up her husband's shoes from in front of his easy chair and started to the bedroom. She noticed he had a hole in the sole of the right one. "Eddie, we need to get these re-soled."

"Yeah, I know but I don't have any time. With me now working at the bank in the morning and for the city in the afternoon, I don't have the time to get it done. Besides, I can't go a day without shoes."

"Maybe I could buy you a new pair."

"Gladys, you don't work. Where would you get the money, unless, I gave it to you? I might as well pick them out myself. Besides, these have never been re-soled—not like the last pair."

"It was just a thought, Eddy. Shoes are too practical anyway. Not personal, like a good gift should be."

"Why do you want to buy me anything? After that first Christmas you never bought me another present."

"The next year I was mad at you because you gave your sister a pretty coat I'd been eyeing at Ava's Dresses for two months. And all you gave me was a sweater."

"Honey, what you don't know is that I bought that coat for you. Then Elizabeth got married and didn't have decent clothes. I took her shopping and bought a couple of dresses, some underwear, and a pair of shoes. On the day of her wedding, it was colder than blip—and she didn't have a coat—so I gave her yours. The next day, the Saturday before Christmas, when you thought I was out with the boys, I hitched a ride to Little Rock and got you that sweater. It took every penny I had."

"Well, what about last year? All you got me last year were some records, and we don't even own a record player."

"Gladys, do you remember your mother calling, saying her toilet wouldn't flush? It had been raining steady for several days. Do you remember?"

"Yes. I think so."

"I spent the entire weekend repairing her system. I had to pawn your present, a record player, to buy the parts I needed. When Christmas Eve came, I went to get the player with money I had earned wrapping presents at the Mercantile. Danny Demeter's father said he'd already sold it. Later, Danny later told me his mother got the nicest record player for Christmas and she was having a great time ordering records through the mail."

"All right, Mr. Too-Good-To-Be-True. You must sit up late at night thinking of likely scenarios that paint a picture showing you as the hardest-working and most under-appreciated man God ever created."

"Gladys, what would you like for Christmas, honey?"

"I don't know. I think I have everything I've ever wanted."

CHAPTER 7 – CHURCH
Sunday morning, December 9, 1945

Merle took off his hat and held it in front with both hands as he walked to an empty pew, He slid to the middle. He knew, before the service started, someone would plop down next to the aisle and that's exactly what Merle wanted.

A piano started playing. Women wore frilly hats. Some men were in dress clothes, others wore starched overalls. This was the Methodist church and it drew from a broad range of the population.

The piano stopped as a man walked to the lectern. He said, "Good Morning."

The congregation responded with a resounding, "Good Morning."

"If you are a visitor, please raise your hand. Brother Smyth and his daughter Amanda are walking down the aisles. They'll give you a brochure for our church. Fill out the back page and drop it into the offering plate. That way we'll have a record of your visit. If you have a special need, write that down as well and we'll mention it in our prayers."

The man turned to the choir. He had a slender stick in his hand and, when he gave it a little flick, the choir members stood. The piano began playing and the choir joined in after a few bars. Merle liked listening to the music. He used a pencil he found stuck in a cylindrical hole on the back of the pew in front of him to fill in the blanks with ficticious data. Sure enough, a couple was now sitting on one end of his pew and a single woman sat on the other end.

After the choir sang its opening song and the congregation joined in for a couple more, a different man stepped to the lectern. He looked out over his flock and said, "I'm so glad to see everyone today. Please bow your heads as I thank the Lord for the blessings he has given us and for the health and welfare of each one of you."

Merle listened to the sermon, nodded a few times, and said "Amen" a couple of times when he agreed with what the preacher had just said. Merle enjoyed himself immensely. After the sermon was finished, the preacher asked the ushers to step forward with one of them blessing the offering. Then, as the choir sang, they went down the aisles passing the plate from one pew to another. The people in each pew put in their offerings and passed the plate down the line. When the usher gave the plate to the man at the end of Merle's pew, Merle got up and walked to get it. He put in his visitor's card and carried it past where he had sat to give to the single woman at the other end. As he walked, he held the plate above the heads of the people seated and, along the way, palmed the large denomination bills he had spied. Easy pickings.

After the service, he shook the preacher's hand and said he had enjoyed the sermon. He said he planned on being back for the evening service and asked what time it started.

CHAPTER 8 – STACY JO
Friday morning, December 14, 1945

Why did he have to be like the others? Boyd was good-looking, well-mannered, and attentive, but after a few days with his heathen friends on the Dancing Deer City Council, and he reverts to a regular jackass.

Stacy Jo had burned Boyd's clothes, severing their relationship forever—or so she thought. The wives of the men on the city council had justifiable complaints and set a course of action Stacy had found funny and went along with, but while the other women were married to the targets of their frustration, she didn't enjoy the same status. So, instead of withholding sex, which was a moot point anyway, she withheld potatoes. She achieved the same goal. But everything backfired when the men took their frustrations to the women of the Gilded Lily.

When Stacy found out, she went crying to her mother in Skunk Hollow, only coming back to Dancing Deer for her final act of revenge and to beg for a few days off from work. She had a key to Boyd's house and gathered all of his clothes and his new pair of hand-made cowboy boots. The same ones he'd had constructed by a craftsman in Fort Worth using outlines of his feet she'd drawn. She piled everything waist-high in a circle in his front yard and, after dousing the mound with coal oil, she burned them to the ground. When she left, Boyd had not one pair of socks nor one pair of underwear. He had no shirts, no pants, no heavy coat, and most certainly no expensive cowboy boots. She left chuckling about her ability to exact vengeance. By the time she had driven the fifteen miles to her mother's house, she was not so sure she had done the right thing.

"Stacy Jo, it's been so nice to have you back. Why don't you find a job in Skunk Hollow? The day before you showed up, a man robbed the bank and that prissy little teller of theirs gave him an entire sack of money. Jumbo Johnny chased him out of the bank and shot him as he ran to a getaway car. Now the bank teller has quit, saying life's too short to have such a dangerous job.

"The bank got most of its money back and gave Jumbo a fifty-dollar reward.

"Stacy, why don't you apply for her job? It's the same work you do for the First Bank and Trust of Dancing Deer." Stacy Jo's mother propped her feet on a hassock.

"I might. From here, it takes thirty minutes to drive that fifteen miles. And when it's raining or ice is on the streets, even longer than that. I think I will. I'll call in Monday morning and extend my time off by another day."

When Stacy Jo graduated from high school, she looked around for a job in Skunk Hollow, but no one was hiring so she tried the town down the road and was hired as a bank teller. That's where, a year later, she met Boyd. He came in and deposited a check. Fifteen minutes later he was back in line and wanted to withdraw some of his deposited money. Then, in thirty minutes, he was back wanting to deposit some of it again, saying he didn't need all he had taken. Two hours later, he was in line to make another withdrawal. When she counted his bills, he suggested she go with him that evening to see a magician's act at the Ritz Grand Hotel and Ballroom. He said he couldn't keep coming back to make withdrawals or deposits for the same dollars. After that, they saw each other regularly and she eventually moved in with a girlfriend so she could be closer to work and to Boyd.

With her relationship with Boyd now down the toilet, she became depressed. All her girlfriends were married. Their husbands were returning from fighting the Germans or the Japanese. They were planning on babies. Stacy Jo thought her life was over. At twenty-three, she was already an old maid. Wrinkles would soon appear. Taut muscles would grow fleshy. Things that looked better standing up would start to sag. She shouldn't have burned his clothes. What if he had a good excuse? She had not even given him the opportunity to explain. What if she had jumped to the wrong conclusion?

"Dear, someone called this morning. He asked if I would give you a message."

"Yes, Mother. What is it?"

"Oh, dear me, I seem to have forgotten. He was a friendly man. Had a pleasing voice. Could he have been your boss, dear?"

"Mother, for heaven's sake, think. Was his name Boyd? Mom, was he Boyd?"

"Yes, it might have been Boyd. Now, what was I was supposed to tell you? He said it was crucial—urgent even. Made me repeat it back. Oh well, I'm sure, if it really was that important, he'll call again. Can I get you something to eat? You're all skin and bones, Stacy Jo. You've been living in Dancing Deer for quite a long time. Haven't you been eating?"

CHAPTER 9 – THE WOMEN
Friday afternoon, December 14, 1945

Clarice stood before the wives of the city council members. "Ladies, our plans backfired. We withheld sex or potatoes because the men made us help pay off their betting losses to Bill. Those rats then went to the Gilded Lily in Skunk Hollow every time they had an urge, and when they came home to us they acted like they weren't all that interested. It's enough to make a woman use a knife to hang a trophy in her kitchen."

"Clarice, you talking about scalping?"

"No, I'm talking about castrating."

"Whew-ee, that's like cutting off your nose to spite your face."

"I didn't mean it literally. I was just making a point." Clarice waited a moment before continuing. "Ladies, now Father O'Reilly has stepped in and complicated matters. We're all getting counseling to reconcile our differences with the men. What we need to discuss today is how we're gonna handle the situation. Do we make up with the men? Do we continue with the hostility? Do we act like nothing happened? What are our choices?"

Betty Baker raised her hand. "Withholding sex was fine at first, but I ended up suffering as much as my John and felt denied every time he suggested we get intimate and I had to fake a headache. When we found out the boys were going to Skunk Hollow, I took the children shopping. What I didn't understand was that our spending spree was using the money my John had set aside for a trip to visit my parents at Christmas. Now, we can't go."

Summer Satterfield said, "Yeah, same with me. When George saw all my packages, he plopped in his chair running his hands through his hair. He told me, because of my revenge, we couldn't afford to buy each other Christmas presents. A week later he handed me the checkbook, and said I was now responsible for paying the bills. It's been a nightmare."

Imogene chimed in with, "I retrieved my mother from a nursing home and gave her the front bedroom. My retaliation against Harold has resulted in catastrophic consequences. I now spend my time taking care of her needs. She has a special diet and is incontinent. And Harold, bless his heart, says we're saving so much money he wants to continue the arrangement. He bought a barbecue grill and thinks he's helping by cooking hamburgers twice a week."

"Harold cooks?"

"Yes, but not well. And he doesn't clean up his mess. His efforts have actually given me more work than when he didn't stir from his recliner until I called him to dinner."

Ophelia Obadiah slowly stood in front of her chair. "I'm sorry, ladies. I might have been the cause of all our problems." The room grew quiet as the attending women waited for Ophelia to explain. "If I had disposed of the powdered rhino horn when I got rid of those other potions none of this would have happened. You see, the damned stuff worked after all. When I sprinkled it on his oatmeal or his eggs or mixed it in his orange juice, he grew big on his way to work—and I didn't know about it.

"I eventually found a bottle of medicine in the cabinet that said it was for Priapism. When I asked Faisal about it. he confessed to having a weird medical condition. He said the doctor looked it up in a reference book and gave him some pills. After I asked if the pills worked, he started crying and said 'No, they're only sedatives. Nothing works. It usually occurs early in the morning and lasts for two to four hours.'"

"What about the time you mixed the powdered rhino horn with ointment in your hand before snugling against his side and slowly sliding you hand inside . . . ?"

"Whoa, let's not elaborate too much. We all know how Ophelia made the last application."

"Faisal told me it was the worst ever. It grew twice as big as before and lasted till lunch. He couldn't leave his counter. He had tears in his eyes when he told me how he kept bumping into everything waist-high. He said he couldn't hide the problem very well and had to tell his female assistant to take the day off."

"Okay. Who's got the catalog?"

"Ladies." Clarice pounded on the lectern. "Ladies, let's not let this get out of hand. If that stuff works, maybe we can use it in some meaningful way to have the last word."

"What sizes does it come in?"

"How are we going to pay for it? I can't use any more family funds."

"Me either. Let's have a bake sale and use the proceeds to buy the large economy size. Then we'll divvy it up and wait until the right moment when everyone can use it at the same time. That'll show the men who's in charge."

CHAPTER 10 – THE MEN
Saturday morning, December 15, 1945

"George, that was a good idea to hire Claude to repair the Gilded Lily. We couldn't do it ourselves with no lumber."

"Yeah, but I wish we could let him do all the work and we didn't have to spend our Saturdays with him telling us what to do."

"I don't mind. This is the cheapest way to get it done and the only way Betts would agree. None of us have the proper skills, but we can follow instructions from someone who does. A few more days like last week and we'll be finished."

The men pulled up in front of the Gilded Lily. The women had arrived earlier in Suzanne's blue coup and Claude had come in his company truck. The women and Claude waited on the men to begin another day of repairing the damage caused by their fight, weeks before, with the men from Skunk Hollow.

Betts walked out of the kitchen with a tray of sweets and a pot of coffee. "I'm sure glad you ladies have come to chaperone the boys. They're a rowdy bunch on their own, but you should have seen them handle the men from Skunk Hollow. They were mostly naked and outnumbered two to one. It was a sight I'll never forget."

Summer Satterfield said, "Naked? I don't suppose you got any pictures?"

"Not me, but one of the girls did. Her name's Twinkie. Always wears pink. She's not up yet, but when she is, we'll get her to display her shots. I had her to blow 'em up into glossy eight by tens. Thought we'd frame and mount 'em on the wall."

"Do the men know about the pictures?"

"Naw. They had their hands full and, other than these repair efforts, they haven't been back. You ladies sure know how to control your men. I have cream and sugar for your coffee. Should I offer some to the men?"

"Hell, no. They're just looking for an excuse to sit down on the job. The only one actually working is Claude. The others bring him things or hold things for him. When they try to do something themselves, he has to take it back apart and fix it properly."

"Well, they might not be quite so good with a hammer, but they sure are good with other things."

"Uh . . . Betts. What are you talking about, specifically?"

"The way they banded together when they whipped all those other men. They fought as a team and the men from Skunk Hollow fought as individuals with no one watching their backs and no one helping a fallen comrade. It was marvelous to watch your men go after it. If they had not been tearing up my house I could have enjoyed it more, but as it was it was still pretty astonishing."

"Good. There for a moment I thought . . . uh, I'm not sure what I thought."

"George, would you put these stiles in? Use a level to make sure each one is straight. That's it. All right Johnston, you need to replace this one board. It wasn't tongue and groove, so you just butted it up against the next board. Eventually, a crack will appear. You need to take it up and use only the boards from that farthest stack. Okay?"

"Yes, sir."

"Claude, do you know how many more Saturdays this is gonna take? It's nine days till Christmas and we still got two storefronts to paint."

"Boyd, if we work hard today, we can get all the construction done and that leaves the sanding, staining, and painting. So I guess, with a little luck, we could finish next Saturday."

A young lady, rubbing the sleep from her eyes, descended the stairs, brushing up against each man she came to. When she got to the bottom and came face to face with Claude, she stopped in her tracks and let out a wild shriek. "Claude, is that you? Claude, I've missed you so much." She put her arms around Claude's neck and kissed him on the mouth. "All the girls wanted to leave with you. Marianne's here, too. Wait till she hears I've found our Claude. The Painted Lady wasn't the same after you left." She turned around and ran back up the stairs. When she brushed against George Satterfield, she grabbed hold of something to steady her step. "You keep that thought in your mind, sugar."

"Uh, Claude. Is there anything you can say to explain that young lady's behavior?"

"I did some repair work on their house in Fort Smith."

"And . . ."

"I tossed out a few hot-heads and installed a security system of lights and buzzers."

"How did you get paid?"

"With money, Harold. They paid me with money." Claude then walked away to count the number of boards and the number of stiles left to install. He hoped one more Saturday and this job would be done.

"Betts, have you seen Marianne? I've found our Claude. I'm so happy."

"Honey, she hasn't gotten here yet." Betts turned to her guests from Dancing Deer. "I've recently expanded. Some of the new girls live in town. I send a car to pick them up each day around noon."

Summer leaned toward Ophelia and Clarice. "Should we tell Adelle? She might want to join the party."

A second woman walked down the stairs wearing a pink robe.

"Is that Twinkie?"

"Yes, let me introduce you."

A few moments later the women had retreated to the kitchen where they looked at six large glossy prints in black and white spread over the countertop.

"My goodness. Faisal is huge." Ophelia quickly flipped over one of the pictures.

Twinkie pointed to another print. "This one is particularly interesting. See how they're in a circle at the bottom of the stairs. Each one pretty much in his altogether, holding out a chair in one hand and a club or stair stile in the other."

Summer said, "Georgie looks like he's ready to do battle with the devil himself. It excites me."

"Would any of you ladies care to purchase your own set of prints? I can get them autographed."

A few minutes later, after another young lady descended the stairs and headed to the parlor, Mayor Bob brought Johnston the remaining boards from the tongue and groove stack. "Damn, this is embarrassing. I have to keep looking down so Clarice won't think I'm making an appointment for later with one of the women."

"Shhh . . . if they're not talking among themselves, they can hear normal conversation. If you say anything, whisper it."

"Right."

The young woman from the Painted Lady walked up to Claude holding out a cup of coffee and a Danish. "Claude, darling. May I sit here and watch you work?"

CHAPTER 11 – CLAUDE
Saturday evening, December 15, 1945

Adelle loved cooking for Claude. He was always appreciative of her efforts. She thought nothing was too good or too extravagant for her man. One night she would cook a steak and the next a rack of lamb. She made flaming desserts, various chocolate concoctions, and stuffed baked potatoes. In fact, stuffed baked potatoes was her personal favorite. Her recipe called for pressing chunky rock salt into the largest white potatoes she could find, then she wrapped each inside resinous brown paper. The wrapped potatoes were baked over a low heat until a toothpick would easily slide through. At that point, she cut through each wrapped potato to spread it wide open. With a fork she removed the soft part of each side, sprinkled her collected treasure with sea salt and coarse black pepper, and mixed it with sour cream, home-churned butter, and chives. Adelle folded it together before stuffing the mixture back into the empty potato skins. At this point, she covered each with slices of mild Colby cheese and crumbled bacon. She finished by putting them back in the oven until the cheese had properly melted. When Claude was told he was having a stuffed potato, his mouth started salivating to the point he couldn't concentrate on the paper he was reading. Adelle never had to call him twice to dinner.

"Claude, how are you coming on repairing the Gilded Lily?"

"One more day—next Saturday—and it's a done deal."

"Darling, next Saturday is the twenty-second. That's three days before Christmas. You're going to work the last Saturday before Christmas? I was hoping we could drive into Little Rock or Fort Smith and do some shopping, take in a show, and have an enjoyable meal at one of their sidewalk cafes."

"Maybe enough of the men could get off a day during the week. I could finish it by myself, but the women want the men to suffer, so they have to be there to bring me things and to hold the nails I hammer.

Today I had them do some things on their own and half were screwed up and had to be re-done."

"Let me talk to the women. Is any particular one in charge?"

"Uh no, you better let me do that. If I can't get them to agree then I'll sic you on 'em."

At this moment, the telephone rang and Adelle excused herself to answer. In a moment she returned saying it was Mayor Bob's wife, Clarice.

To Adelle, Claude said, "Nothing like prompt service."

"Claude, we need to talk. Can you meet with me and some of the ladies this evening?"

"I'm having supper right now. Where did you want to meet?

"How about that little diner out on the highway? We won't take much of your time."

"Okay. In an hour?"

"An hour will be fine."

"Hello, ladies."

Clarice Springer, Ophelia Obadiah, and Betty Baker huddled together in a small booth separated from the remaining customers by one that was empty. In unison they said, "Hello, Claude."

"Have you eaten?"

"Of course he's eaten. He was eating when I called."

"Would you like something to drink?"

"No. What's so urgent?"

"It's the men."

"Uh, oh."

"They told us they went to the Gilded Lily to initiate Boyd into some sort of man's fraternal bliss."

"And . . ."

"And one of the girls took pictures of them fighting the men from Skunk Hollow."

"You already knew that."

"Claude, they were naked. One wore a t-shirt. Two were wearing long-handled underwear, and Boyd—Boyd was fully clothed. He wasn't even missing a shoe. The rest were jaybirding it."

"So now you know the truth. Something you probably knew all along."

"Maybe, but what we didn't know about was the pictures. Twinkie snapped six and Betts had her blow them up to eight by tens. They're planning on framing them for hanging on the wall."

"Ha, ha. Oh, sorry ladies."

"Claude, we've got to figure a way to steal those negatives—and the prints. Twinkie asked if we might like to purchase our own set. She thinks she's sitting on something valuable."

"We thought about snatching them but, without the negatives, it would have been a counterproductive effort."

"Did you offer to buy the negatives, as well as the prints?"

"No. That's not the way we do things."

"So you want me to steal the negatives?"

"Yep."

"I don't think so. I'd lose too much if I got caught."

"We'd make it worth your while."

"What do you have in mind?"

"Whatever you want."

"I don't want anything I don't already have."

"Does Adelle know about the Painted Lady?"

"Yes. We don't harbor any secrets."

"Damn. Does she also know how those prostitutes from Fort Smith fawn all over you?"

Claude thought a moment before he said, "When a man shows up who treats them like human beings, someone who actually listens to what they have to say, they go crazy over him. I was the caretaker of their house and you would have thought I was a king in some foreign land. The johns who aren't mean treat the attractive ones like beautiful toys, to discard when the newness wears off. They treat the ones a little older or a little more plain, with disdain. No kind words, not even an acknowledgment they're there." Claude took a drink of water. "I was just kind to the ladies."

"Is there not anything we can do to make you change your mind?"

"Okay, ladies, here's what I'll do. If you really want those negatives . . . ."

"And the prints."

"All right—and the prints. I'll figure a plan you ladies can use to steal them. I'll show you how to do it and even help each person learn her part in the plot. So, how badly do you ladies want those negatives?"

"And the prints."

"Ophelia, is there something on those photos you find particularly embarrassing?"

"Yes, I do. I played a dirty trick on Faisal and the poor guy was exhibiting the effects of my efforts for all the world to see. I'm mortified and embarrassed for my husband."

"Ophelia, what did you do?"

"Claude, I . . . I . . . uh, I gave him powdered rhino horn in his cereal, on his eggs, in his oatmeal . . ."

"Don't forget the time you reached under the covers to slather it on with your hand after he was sound asleep."

"Does that stuff really work?"

"If you saw the picture, you wouldn't have any doubt in your mind."

"Sounds like we need to steal the prints and negatives and then destroy them."

"That's acceptable with us."

"Okay, let me think on it. Let's plan on finishing the work on Wednesday. Since I'm doing most of the work anyway, a few of you ladies could take the place of the men, a few others could keep Betts occupied while Ophelia steals the negatives and the prints. The ladies working need to wear something they can get dirty. Sanding and staining will probably cause you to trash what you're wearing when you get home. So a pair of your husband's old work pants and an old shirt would be the order of the day."

"That's great, Claude. Let's shake on it."

CHAPTER 12 – BOYD
Sunday afternoon, December 16, 1945

"No, Stacy Jo is not here. Yes, I told her you called. She's not been feeling well. Must be the chicken-pox or something. I'll tell her you called. Yes, okay . . . and the same to you." Stacy's mother hung up the receiver. "Funny man. Of course, I told Stacy Jo he called."

Boyd was upset. Just when he was getting accustomed to having a woman around the house and now there's no woman. Sure he was mad for her burning his clothes, but then again, she had good reason. A man in a serious relationship should not do anything so dishonorable as to visit a bordello. What had he been thinking? He wanted to make amends. He wanted Stacy Jo to come back. Maybe he should bite the bullet and ask her to marry him. No, that was too much appeasement. Probably a little urging on the telephone would be sufficient.

"No, Stacy Jo is still not here. I look for her any minute. Do you have a message I could give her?" A pause. "I most certainly did. She said she didn't know who you were." A second pause. "This is Gerald, right?" Another pause. "So now we have two men trying to get in touch with my Stacy Jo. Lloyd said he worked with her and he loved her. Are you telling me you're in love with her too? It's a wonder she found time for both of you. What do they say in merchandising, 'the first one with the money?' Oh, what was the rest of that saying? Well, thank you for calling, Boyd. If you see Lloyd, tell him Stacy Jo is staying the night with her high school . . . oh, forget that, I wasn't supposed to mention that to anyone. Good-bye, Boyd."

After the telephone call Boyd didn't move from his chair. What's going on? Stacy has another boyfriend? Someone who works at the bank? That's preposterous. When did she have time? Must've been when he went out with his buddies. So every time he was visiting the

Gilded Lily she was tarnishing something else. I got to find out who this Lloyd is. Boyd dialed his best friend.

"Hello Betty, may I speak with Johnston?" A pause. "Johnston, do you know anybody at the bank named Lloyd?"

"Yeah, he's that kid they hired from Cakebread. I think he works in the loan department. Does title checks and research on liens at the courthouse. Nice looking guy. Why, what's up?"

"Damn. All the time I was seeing Stacy Jo, she was two-timing me with this Lloyd. And . . . and now she's two-timing both of us with a third guy she used to go to school with."

"Man, that's cold."

"Think I ought to tell Lloyd?"

"Boyd, you shouldn't make decisions like that until you've had a chance to think about it—and to cool off a bit. Then, if you want to tell Lloyd, me and the boys will go with you. You know—in case he's into martial arts or something."

"That makes me feel a lot better. I don't know what I'd do without friends like you. Thanks, Johnston."

CHAPTER 13 – LLOYD
Monday morning, December 17, 1945

Lloyd Garrison was hired by Charles Jimmerson, right out of high school. He'd graduated at the top of his class, but there were no jobs in the little town of Cakebread, so he went twenty miles south to Dancing Deer, the county seat of Marsden County. He first applied at the newspaper but was told there were not any openings, then he went to the courthouse where Judge Murphy McAdams had just hired a summer intern. His next stop was the First Bank and Trust of Dancing Deer. There he met the new general manager and, after filling out an application and sitting through a short interview, he was offered a job.

Lloyd saved half of each paycheck and hoped to have enough money to pay his first semester's tuition and lodging by September. But that was three months previous. He'd had to put it off. He would start at the University of Arkansas in Fayetteville after the new year began, with the beginning of the spring semester.

Charles Jimmerson said banks were always looking for bright young men with degrees in finance or accounting. What Lloyd really wanted was to get a degree in jurisprudence and work for Mr. Michael Jellico. He'd met Jellico at the courthouse when he was trying to determine if a man borrowing money from the bank held a clear title to his farm. After a little chit-chat with Jellico, Lloyd asked around and found everyone was of the same opinion. Jellico was the finest lawyer in Arkansas—several levels better than their district attorney.

A knock on his closet door and a man came in. "Lloyd, there's someone who wants to see you. Several men actually. One is Mayor Bob. Do you want me to bring them back?"

Lloyd looked over his boss's shoulder. Several men gathered in the doorway and in the hall leading to his closet.

He got up from his chair and walked to the door. He held out his hand to the man in front. "Lloyd Garrison. I'd offer you gentlemen seats but my office is really a storage closet they cleaned out. There's no room for additional chairs."

"No problem. Just wanted to give you a heads up. Our woman's two-timing us with her sweetheart from high school."

"I beg your pardon."

"You're Lloyd, right?"

"Yes."

"From Cakebread?"

"Yes."

"I'm Boyd, and Stacy Jo is a two-timing broad. A couple of weeks ago she burned my clothes and ran off to Skunk Hollow where her other boyfriend lives."

"I never meant . . ."

"It doesn't matter. I just thought you ought to know." With that, Boyd turned and led his troop of buddies through the foyer and outside.

Shaken, Lloyd had to sit in his chair. He wondered out loud, "Now how did Boyd know about me and Stacy?"

CHAPTER 14 – SKUNK HOLLOW STAKEOUT
Monday noon, December 17, 1945

"I think he thought you was about to pulverize him."

"Yeah, he was shaking in his boots. Probably, thought him and Stacy Jo had kept it sufficiently hush-hush. I bet he's calling her right now."

Boyd cocked his head with lips pinched together. "He sure was young."

"Yeah, I like 'em young too. Guess it's no different with dames. Get a young stallion while his hormones are raging, clamp a leg around him . . ."

"Good Lord, Bob. I don't even want to think about that picture you're making me think about." Boyd shuffled his feet. "Boys, I'm going to Skunk Hollow and see if I can find this other guy."

"You want we should come along?"

"No. No telling how long it'll take. She's probably living with him and will just return home occasionally to check on her mother or to get a little laundry done."

"We need to get back to work anyhow. Johnston, did you convince those last two merchants their storefronts will look better having their bricks washed and only the trim painted."

"Yes, I did. Boyd and I washed them this morning. If we work on the painting this afternoon, we could then be done with the entire package."

"I'm for that. The women said they'd go with Claude and help him finish the Gilded Lily on Wednesday. So men, we will soon be through and have things back to normal. Even the women are coming around."

"Yeah, but Father O'Reilly has another lecture or two."

"Small price to pay. Imogene has been more civil to me than at any time in the past ten years."

"Yeah, I can tell a similar story. There's been a remarkable improvement in Clarice's behavior just since Saturday."

"You can't credit the Father with that. We haven't had a session since long before Saturday."

"Maybe not, but she's had to work on those written exercises he gave us. Johnston, you got ours done?"

"Yeah, I've already given it to Harold. He'll pass it on. It's Rube's turn to do the next one."

"Teamwork, that's how we stay a step ahead of the women."

"I agree."

"Boyd, what you gonna do when you find this third guy?"

"I don't know. But I got to find him so I can put Stacy Jo out of my head."

"Okay. We'll meet at those last two businesses as soon as we can after work, Everyone in agreement?"

"Yeah."

"I'll be there."

"Me too."

Boyd parked his car across the street and down two doors from Stacy Jo's family home. He had a good view and there were two more cars parked on the street so he didn't think he'd stand out. However, what Boyd had not noticed was that there was an alley behind the houses with each house having a backyard driveway opening onto it. So when Stacy Jo went somewhere, or came home from somewhere, she used the alley. She entered a block away and came in and left her house through the back door. Boyd watched the front. Only visitors used the front. Boyd was in for a long wait.

Wrapped in a blanket Boyd slept in his car for the rest of that day and night. He left only long enough to eat and visit restrooms. His beard grew, his legs ached, and he began to develop a . . . well, let's just say he needed a bath. Early Tuesday afternoon, Stacy Jo's mother went outside to check her mailbox. She walked over to Boyd's car and knocked on his window.

When Boyd rolled down the window, she said, "You waiting for Stacy Jo?"

"Uh . . . yes, ma'am. I am."

"Come inside and I'll fix you a cup of coffee. You'll freeze out here. They say it's going to start snowing again."

"Thank you, ma'am. I was prepared to wait as long as it took."

"You'll be more comfortable in the house. Come along young man."

Inside, Stacy Jo's mother had a fire going in the fireplace. Boyd walked over to warm his hands. In a minute he removed his jacket and backed up to the heat source. A few minutes later, his pants legs were too hot to touch the calves of his legs. He gingerly moved a few feet farther away from the fire.

"Young man, here's something to warm you up. May I take your coat? Are you Lloyd? No, Gerald, then? No, how about Patrick? No, then, who are you? Those are the only boyfriends I know about."

"I'm Boyd."

"Hmm, Boyd. I don't recall her talking about a Boyd. You sure it's Stacy Jo and not Geraldine from across the street. You waiting to see her?"

"No, it's Stacy Jo. She works at the bank in Dancing Deer."

"Yes. That's her. But now she works in Skunk Hollow."

"When did that happen?"

"Monday. She gave her notice today. Have you had breakfast?"

"No, ma'am."

"Is the coffee strong enough for you? I can never remember how much to put in. There's sweet cream in the refrigerator and sugar on the table. I'll get my apron and fix you something. It's been a long time since I've had a man in the house."

"Ma'am, I've been in the car for two days. Would you mind if I used your bathroom to freshen up while we wait for Stacy Jo?"

"You go right ahead. I'll get you some whiskey and molasses for those sniffles. Or maybe that's for coughing. I can never keep things like that straight. Take your time. I'll fix you a nice hot breakfast."

Boyd hadn't thought to pack any clothes or a shaving kit. So he opened the medicine cabinet to see if there might be something he could use. There was a knock on the bathroom door. Boyd walked over and, holding onto the door handle, lowered his head toward the door. "Yes?"

"Throw out your clothes and I'll wash them for you. I've got clean towels."

Boyd opened the door barely enough to transact business with Stacy Jo's mother. Perched on top of the towels sat a small box.

"That's my late husband's toiletries. If you can use any of his stuff you're welcome to do so." When she left, she took Boyd's clothes.

Boyd locked the door. Then he put a new blade in a safety razor and lathered his face with soap. Forty-five minutes later he emerged wrapped in a towel.

"You want to put on some of Edgar's clothes? Yours won't be dry for a while."

"Thank you, ma'am."

"You may call me Joyce. It's nice to have someone to talk to."

Boyd took the clothes and went back into the bathroom. In a few minutes, he emerged. The clothes were several sizes too large, but Boyd felt reasonably comfortable and set in a big chair in front of the fireplace. The fire cracked, sizzled, and popped. Through the front window, he could see it was now snowing.

"Joyce, did Stacy Jo go back to work today?"

"Yes, after a nice vacation."

"How long before we can expect her?"

"I don't know, dear. I don't have a clock in the house and have given up trying to wind my internal one. I sleep whenever I feel like it. I eat whenever I get hungry. I check the mail every day—sometimes two or three times because I can't remember if I've already been outside. I look out the window and determine what time of year it is by the color of the leaves. Today it's snowing so it must be winter."

"Next week is Christmas."

"Oh, dear me. I'll have to remember to get Stacy Jo something. Come along I've got your breakfast fixed."

Boyd looked at his watch. It was two o'clock in the afternoon. After Boyd had finished a late breakfast, he and Joyce played checkers.

"Young man, you have to take your jump."

"I don't want to. If I jump that checker, you'll jump three of mine." Boyd reluctantly picked up a checker, advanced it over another of a different color, and sat it down on an empty square. "It's a good thing we're not playing for money. You've won every game. In the last, I didn't get a man across the center line. How'd you get so good?"

"My husband was a checker champion. He'd warm up on me before tournaments. When someone came here to play him, he'd say, 'You play her first. If you can beat her, then we'll play. If you can't beat her, you'd be wasting my time.'" Joyce lifted a checker, jumped three times in a convoluted manner, and picked up the captured pieces.

"Did you ever win against him?"

"Never won a game until there at the end."

CHAPTER 15 – LOOKING FOR BOYD
Tuesday morning, December 18, 1945

Stacy Jo gave her notice to Charles Jimmerson, saying she'd found a job at the Skunk Hollow bank. She said she needed to be closer to her mother, who was in failing health. Charles took his list of employees and immediately started to mentally rearrange cover for Stacy Jo until he could find a permanent replacement.

Stacy's friends began planning a farewell party and Lloyd offered to take her to lunch. She didn't see Boyd. In fact, she hadn't seen Boyd since Thanksgiving when they were in the serving line dishing food to the poor and the displaced. Dancing Deer didn't have starving people so she stretched out her arms and needy people were bussed in from neighboring towns.

What's with Lloyd? Every time she looked his way he had a silly grin on his face.

That afternoon she drove to Boyd's house. After parking in the circular driveway, Stacy slowly walked past the flowers she had planted last Spring. No one had been there to protect them from the freezing cold. She checked her key. It still worked. She opened the door and stepped inside. Boyd was not the messiest man she knew, but he was far from the neatest as well. No trash in the kitchen. Either he had just carried it out or he had been eating all his meals in cafes. In the bedroom, she found the bed un-made with new clothes strewn around the room. She gathered the clothes and made the bed, putting on fresh sheets.

After working hard all day and answering a thousand questions from her co-workers, she looked forward to crawling back to Boyd and asking his forgiveness. She was exhausted and plopped down on the divan after turning on the radio. During the next couple of hours, she got up only to turn up the heat and to see if the refrigerator held anything she could fix. When Boyd got home, she wanted his evening meal prepared. Maybe she'd wait a moment before groveling at his feet. He might be the one to ask forgiveness first. She'd already decided that if he did, he wouldn't have to ask twice. She might not let him finish asking the first time. And if he hesitated, she'd go first. She had a lot invested in Boyd and she didn't want that investment to go to waste. After all, Boyd was smart and sweet and kind and . . . and what was she saying? He went to the Gilded Lily, for God's sakes. The man's a cretin. Stacy gathered herself and ran out the door to her car. She barely remembered to lock the front door.

It was seven in the evening. Where was Boyd? She drove to Snockered, the town pool hall and honky-tonk on the road to Jasper just outside the city limits. His truck wasn't there and, since it wasn't at his house, he had to be in it somewhere. She drove to the diner on the highway and to the little cafe on Main Street. Then she drove to the Ritz Bistro, where she parked and went inside. The *maître d'* said Boyd had not been there, but he had been there every night for a couple of weeks.

Stacy drove home wondering where Boyd could be.

When she got home, the house was dark and her mother already in bed. Stacy went to the bathroom, brushed her teeth, removed her makeup, and slipped into a flannel nightshirt. She crawled into bed under four quilts. With only smoldering ashes in the front room's fireplace, the house was decidedly cold.

That night she slept fitfully, tossing and turning; that is, she tossed and turned while pinned under four quilts, which translates into not much tossing and turning after all.

CHAPTER 16 – ADELLE
Tuesday evening, December 18, 1945

"Adelle? Is this Adelle Peterson?"

"Yes. Who's this?"

"Claude has a woman at the Gilded Lily. Thought you'd like to know." Click.

"Hello. Who is this? Hello. Is this Gena?"

"Hello, Rupert. I'm trying to get a hold of Claude. Do you know where he might be?"

"He called an hour ago and asked if I needed the truck tomorrow. He didn't say where he was going or why he needed it."

"Okay, thank you, Rupert. Uh, Rupert, he didn't say not to say anything did he?"

"Nope. Acted like everything was fine. You and Claude having problems?"

"Oh, no. Nothing like that. Thanks, Rupert."

"Emmett, thank you for coming right over. Do you mind driving to Skunk Hollow? I think Claude might be at the Gilded Lily. And if he is, he's broken a promise."

"Man, I hope he's there. I've missed you, Adelle. I haven't been with another woman since we broke up."

"Emmett, we're just friends. If Claude is there, it doesn't mean you and I will be a couple again. It just means Claude and I are having a problem of our own."

"Okay, but it's a start."

For the next thirty minutes, Emmett Irving made small talk to the best of his abilities with a distraught Adelle Peterson. As they traveled down the winding road, Emmett thought how nice it would be to have Adelle beside him all the time. He thought again about using her money to finance his run for the governorship. Damn, why couldn't she see the opportunity like he did? Well, he was given an opening and this time he wasn't going to fritter it away. This time he'd make the most of it.

"Adelle, do you know where the Gilded Lily is? I mean, I've never been there. I've only been to Skunk Hollow a couple of times and I don't think it's in town."

"No. I was counting on you. We'll have to ask someone. Let's drive into town and ask a waitress. They're privy to all the gossip . . . they and beauty shop operators."

When Adelle and Emmett arrived at the Gilded Lily, Claude's truck, with Calhoun Construction Co. painted on its side, was parked in front.

"Okay, he's here. What now?"

"Emmett, go inside and see what he's doing."

"A man in politics can't be seen in a place like this. It could ruin a career." Emmett waited a moment and continued with, "But I'll make an exception for you, Adelle."

"Just poke your head in, scope out the place, and see if Claude is there. And if he is, find out what the hell he's doing."

"You got it."

Emmett opened the car door and slowly walked the thirty or forty steps to the front door. A woman must have seen him coming because when he reached for the handle, the door swung open. A sultry voice asked him to step inside.

"Ever been here before, sugar?"

"No."

"Step in here." The woman pointed to an adjacent room. "Betts likes to welcome all first-timers herself."

"But, I just want to see if Claude Calhoun, a friend of mine, is here. His truck's outside. I'm not interested in . . . uh, that's not a place your hand ought to be."

"Just checking you out, sugar. Claude's here all right, but you got to see Betts before you get to go in—just looking or not."

"Will it cost me anything?"

"Not unless you see something you like. I have a little time and could take care of you in a way you've never experienced."

"I . . . uh . . . I . . ."

"Betts, here's a new dude." She turned back to Emmett, "I'll be in the parlor. Come see me."

Another woman stepped from a dark doorway and reached out a hand. "I'm Betts, the madam of the Gilded Lily. If this is your first time, you'll have to show some identification, get checked by a nurse, and set up an account."

"I don't want to give you any identification. I don't have a disease. I don't want an account. In fact, I don't even want to be here." Emmett bolted from the room and, four strides later, left through the front door. He ran to his car and plopped down in the driver's seat. With sweat dripping from his brow onto his glasses, Emmett said, "Adelle, he's there all right. Had an arm around one girl and another was astraddle his knee feeding him grapes. I don't think he saw me. I'm lucky to have escaped with my pants still on. We need to leave before the police come and raid the place."

"Emmett, why don't we move the car to a dark area under the trees where we can keep an eye on the front door and still see Claude's truck. If he doesn't come out in thirty minutes, you can take me home."

CHAPTER 17 – MARIANNE
Wednesday morning, December 19, 1945

It was still dark when Stacy Jo's alarm went off. She stumbled down the hall to the bathroom and spent the next forty-five minutes collecting her wits. Halfway through the shower she'd decided that today she would find Boyd. He might be hiding under a rock, but today she would pick up that rock and pull him out. There was no place he could hide where she would not look. She would ferret him out come hell or high water.

At work on Wednesday, December 19th, Stacy Jo asked everyone she knew, and everyone who knew Boyd, where he was. Johnston Baker came in with a deposit and said Boyd was looking for her. That was preposterous. He knew where she was.

At lunch, Lloyd asked if he could take her to get a bite to eat and winked when he asked. Stacy Jo thought she might eventually have to slap Lloyd. Then several of her co-workers offered to take her to lunch, and when she accepted, Lloyd asked if he could tag along.

Right after work, Stacy Jo went to the grocery store and bought enough food to prepare an excellent meal for Boyd. She fixed fried potatoes, mashed potatoes, new potatoes in melted butter, scalloped potatoes with red onions and sliced bell peppers, and baked potatoes wrapped in aluminum foil, She also fixed a ribeye steak and opened a bottle of a red Bordeaux wine. She lit candles and placed them in the center of the table. She even tuned the radio to Perry Como. When everything was ready, she lay back on his divan and waited.

An hour later and he still had not shown up. Where was Boyd? The only place she had not looked was the Gilded Lily. Stacy Jo blew out the candles and, pulling out of his driveway, threw gravel with her back tires. She was headed to the Gilded Lily, the only rock left to look under.

Claude began the day by driving Ophelia to Skunk Hollow. "Are you up to this, Ophelia?"

"Yes, I think so. I've got those stockings you told me to bring and an entire shoebox of make-up."

"And a wig?"

"I had a hard time finding a wig, but at Gena's Cut and Curl, they had to supply a customer with one after she lost her hair to a permanent gone bad. Gena fixed it in a hairstyle she called 'the floozy.'"

"Perfect."

"Claude, I'm a little scared. What if some creep plops down his money and says, 'Babe, let's crawl in bed'?"

"Tell him you're only there for looks. It's the wrong time for you."

"That's good. I never thought of that."

When they pulled into Skunk Hollow, Claude drove to the other side of town and stopped in front of a boarding house. The snow had stopped and the sun was now warming up the morning. A woman sat in a thick robe on the front porch holding a cup of tea. She stood when Claude and Ophelia walked up.

"Ophelia, this is Marianne. Marianne was at the Painted Lady while I was the caretaker. Marianne, this is Ophelia."

"Pleased to meet you, honey." Marianne held out her hand. "Claude's too modest. He was a lot more than a caretaker. He was the man." Claude gave Marianne a stern look and she changed strides.

"Ophelia, this is not going to be difficult. There's been a regular round-robin of girls these last few weeks. We all get paid according to the tokens we give to Betts each morning. So, she doesn't keep up with who's doing what with whom. It's all business to Betts. She buys the tokens from us for five dollars each. The men buy them from her for ten so the house makes the difference, five dollars per trick.

Saucy and I will help any way we can. One of us will be downstairs, keeping up with Twinkie while the other is at the top of the stairs. While Twinkie is busy downstairs, you replace the negatives and prints with the ones Claude gave you. If it looks like someone is about to go up the stairs with our girl, I'll give the sign and, if there's enough time, Saucy will open the door to tell you. You'll have to leave right then. If there's not enough time, she'll knock on the door. You'll have to slip over to the adjoining bedroom, go to the shower, or find some other place to hide."

"I think I got it."

"We have a couple of hours before the car arrives. Would you like a cup of tea? Then, we'll start on your make-up."

CHAPTER 18 – BOYD IN A QUANDARY
Wednesday mid-morning, December 19, 1945

"Young man, wake up. I've got your breakfast ready."

"I'm sorry, ma'am. You fixed that wonderful meal and I got drowsy sitting next to the fire. Guess I fell asleep."

"Twern't no problem. Stacy Jo came during the night, slept in her bed, and has already left. You missed her."

"I what? She had to walk right by the sofa to get to her bedroom."

"She couldn't have seen you; since you were buried deep under the covers."

"I know. You didn't have any heat on last night."

"Because you didn't put any wood on the fire."

"Okay. There's no arguing with you."

"Trained by the best."

"Edgar the best?"

"Yes, he was."

Boyd went down the hall to the bathroom, brushed his teeth with a lime-colored toothbrush. He bypassed the one in Edgar's bag of toiletries, thinking the lime toothbrush might belong to Stacy Jo since her mother had another bathroom off the master bedroom.

"Young man, your clothes are beside the door. You gonna wait until the food gets cold?"

"No, ma'am. I'll be right there."

Boyd opened the door, picked up his clothes, and started to change. He dropped his clothes to the floor and walked out in Edgar's. "Think I'll eat and then take a shower. Would you like for me to take you shopping so you can buy a Christmas present for Stacy Jo?"

"Young man, that would be wonderful."

"You forget my name?"

"Uh . . . just misplaced it."

"I'm Boyd."

"Thank you, Boyd. Do you love my Stacy Jo?"

"Yes, I do."

"Good. Let's buy her something special. She's all I have."

"She's all I want."

After spending the morning eating breakfast, shaving, bathing, and scraping the snow off the front porch and sidewalk, Boyd walked in with an armload of firewood.

"Boyd, you are a hard worker. Here, drink this coffee while I get my coat."

They drove the few blocks to the shopping area of Skunk Hollow, which happened to be a few stores downtown, and parked. The merchants had tried to clear the snow from in front of their doors and sidewalks so customers could make it in to spend a few hard-earned dollars. They entered a dry-goods store where Stacy Jo's mother picked out four yards of a pretty yellow fabric and a pattern. She said she liked to make her clothes, but Stacy Jo was so finicky about the way she dressed that Joyce had long ago decided store-bought dresses were the only way to go with Stacy Jo.

"Young man," Joyce looked at a piece of paper in the palm of her hand. "Uh . . . Boyd, do you attend church?"

"Occasionally. My best friends are Catholic and I sometimes go with them."

"Stacy Jo doesn't go very often either. She professes her belief but says the church is full of hypocrites. She also says she doesn't get much out of the sermons. I tend to agree. Our minister stutters. Sometimes you want to jump out of the pew and run up front to pat him on the back. Sometimes I want to yell out the word he's having trouble with. It would be sad if it weren't so funny.

"I once listened to Mark Twain speak. He was sitting in a chair on stage telling a story. Now, there's a man who could hold an audience's attention. He started off talking about one story and halfway through somehow digressed to another and when he had introduced the new characters and new scene and new plot, he introduced a third story and was off and running with it. He then mixed up all three stories until we didn't know the location, the time frame, or relationship between the characters. Everyone wanted to help him out. Then he started pulling his stories apart and finished all three, to the amazement of everyone there.

It was the most incredible thing I've ever heard. Well, I don't mean any one of the three stories were incredible by themselves, but it was the way he blended them together, then pulled them back apart and finished each one. I'm glad no one in the audience said anything to him while he had them mixed together. We listen to our minister the same way, hoping he'll eventually make his point and dismiss us."

"Joyce, do they have a jewelry store in Skunk Hollow?"

"I don't think so."

"Then what do you say about letting me take you to Dancing Deer? We've got a lot more shops than Skunk Hollow and there are two stores in particular I think we ought to check out. Then I'll buy you a meal in the best restaurant in northern Arkansas."

"Let's do it."

First they went to Creighton's Jewelry. While Joyce was busy having Meredith Creighton take her picture with her arm draped around a life-sized poster of a man in uniform, Boyd transacted a deal with Mr. Creighton. Soon Boyd received a small package neatly wrapped in red paper encircled with purple ribbon.

The second shop was Ava's Dresses, where Joyce bought Stacy Jo a multi-colored silk scarf and a black leather purse. Boyd paid for them to be wrapped. While they waited Lloyd and Edwin Stanky entered. Lloyd wore a business suit and Ed cut a dashing appearance in a navy blue police uniform. Ed had a briefcase chained to his wrist. The two men greeted Boyd and Joyce, shook Boyd's hand, then retreated to the back room with Ava.

"Boyd, you'll have to bring me shopping here again. This is a fantastic store."

"Are you ready to get something to eat?"

"I am. Have you noticed it's started snowing again?"

"I have. But it's supposed to snow. It's Christmas."

At the Ritz Bistro, the *maître d'* sat them at a table by one of the front windows so they could enjoy the warmth of the restaurant and observe the shoppers carrying packages covered in gaily colored paper. The snow had turned to slush in the street; no one seemed to mind; everyone was in good spirits. Whenever an opening in the crowd appeared a homeless man, wearing a top hat, scraped the slush from the sidewalk into the street.

"Boyd, I don't know when I've had more fun. Can you suggest something from the menu? I don't eat much red meat."

"How about chicken *cordon bleu*? They take a chicken breast and flatten it out, wrap it around a cheese filling, and bread it. Then they bake or deep fry it and serve it covered with a creamy cheese and tomato sauce."

"Whew that sounds rich. Will you be mad at me if I don't eat it all?"

"Absolutely not. However, there are lots of other menu items. Some people just eat the vegetables. They have asparagus tips covered in a béarnaise sauce, purple hull peas, cream peas, broccoli covered with a hollandaise sauce, French-cut green beans, English peas with small onion pearls, marinated mushrooms, and an assortment of soups. I especially like their corn chowder."

"So if I had the chicken, would I get a vegetable as well?"

"Joyce, you can have anything you want."

"Then I'd like the chicken with asparagus tips and a cup of corn chowder."

The waiter took their order, with Boyd ordering a small prime rib with horseradish sauce and a baked potato covered with butter, sour cream, and broken bits of bacon.

"And what would the madam like to drink?"

"Iced coffee."

"And for you, sir?"

"Make that two iced coffees."

"Thank you, sir."

After the meal, they drove to the edge of town and purchased a small Christmas tree. Joyce said she had a box of ornaments in her attic.

"You know, I haven't had a Christmas tree since Edgar died. Boyd, this is a special Christmas, isn't it?"

"Yes, ma'am. It is. I don't expect there ever to be another like it."

CHAPTER 19 – THE STAIRCASE
Wednesday late morning, December 19, 1945

When Claude arrived after dropping off Ophelia, he was surprised when he carried his tools inside. Adelle had joined the women.

"I thought about calling last night. I reasoned that if I wanted you to be with me on Saturday, then you absolutely had to finish today. So I hitched a ride and have worn clothes I could work in. I want to help. Just tell me what to do."

While Betts was occupied with Clarice Springer, Suzanne Abernathy, and Imogene Greenleaf, he planned on sanding, removing the collected dust, staining, and varnishing the flooring and steps. Then he needed to paint the handrail, stiles, and balustrade. He had Adelle, Betty Baker, and Summer Satterfield as helpers.

"Ladies, I have aprons, goggles, and painter's hats for each of you."

Summer said, "Claude, I'll wear the apron but you can keep the goggles and that silly cap."

"It'll keep the paint and varnish out of your hair and the dust out of your eyes."

"I'll be careful."

Betty Baker also declined, and Adelle sided with Summer and Betty so she would not be the only woman there wearing those funny-looking things. Adelle held up the hat. "It sure has a short bill. Not much of a cap, not like a baseball cap."

"Okay, what we're going to do first is sand everything down. But even before we do that we're going to spread paper on the floor to catch most of the dust. Just let me move the hall furniture into one of the rooms. Betts, I'll need for your girls to stay off the stairs for a while."

"Sure. I'll also wait before sending the car for the girls in town. No need in them being here if they can't take the johns upstairs. In fact, I'll put a sign on the door saying we're not opening until this evening."

Claude thought, well, there is the first problem rearing its head.

The staircase extended into the expansive foyer, so the women spread the paper around it in four directions. Then each, with sanding blocks and sheets of sand paper, commenced working on the staircase, much like mother-nature worked on the pyramids.

Several times Claude had to stop their work to tell them not to gouge the wood and to sand back and forth in a single direction with the grain. He had Adelle sand the stiles while he worked on the balustrade.

At lunch, they stopped to eat the sandwiches the three women not working with Claude had prepared at Claude's truck. They lowered Claude's tailgate and used it as a work area. Soon they sat in various chairs on the porch eating chicken-salad sandwiches, coleslaw, and baked beans covered with strips of sliced bacon. They had brought sweet tea and lemonade to drink and pecan pie for dessert. It was a meal relished by a hard-working group of women and one very hard-working man. The sky was beginning to darken, threatening to snow again.

Three women wore pretty dresses. Three other women, wearing men's pants and flannel shirts, were covered from head to toe in sawdust. Adelle ran her fingers through her hair, creating a small dust storm.

"Claude, is it too late to reconsider the cap and goggles?"

"Certainly not."

By mid-afternoon, they wrapped up. Claude carried his tools and the cans of stain, paint, and varnish to his truck. Clarice walked beside him. "How are we gonna get Ophelia back?"

"You need to park off to one side. Hunker down so no one thinks there's anyone in the car. When she's got the negatives and prints, she'll say she's going to step onto the porch for some fresh air and then, when no one's looking, she'll run to an open car door."

"How will she know we're still here waiting for her?"

"Saucy will tell her for you." Claude looked over Clarice's shoulder at Adelle approaching from the front porch. "How were you gonna transport seven women in Suzanne's coupe?"

"Seven? With Ophelia we have six. We met Emmitt Irving leaving as we drove up. He must've given Adelle a lift, as she was already here when we arrived. You know, Claude, you're quite intelligent to figure all this out. It's a shame I'm already married."

Claude reached behind Clarice and took Adelle's hand. "Clarice, I'm spoken for."

Adelle gave his hand an affectionate squeeze. It was what she'd been wanting to hear.

Claude turned to Adelle, "I've got one more chore and then I'll be ready to go. I think you'll be more comfortable in my truck with just me than in Clarice's coupe with five other women."

"I'll be right here."

Claude walked to the Gilded Lily with a red-faced Clarice following close behind and a curious Adelle creeping up, wondering what Claude's last chore might be.

CHAPTER 20 – AN OLD TESTAMENT LESSON
Wednesday afternoon, December 19, 1945

Ophelia sat in a wicker chair with her hands clutching a cup of warm tea. She wondered if Betts would recognize her. She would be wearing heavy makeup and a wig. Maybe she should try to disguise her voice. Once, in a school play, she was cast in a man's role and had to lower her voice an octave to be believable. It hadn't been too hard to do. Other than that, the only thing she could think of was to keep her distance.

"Whatcha thinking about, honey?" Marianne added more eye shadow.

"Just wondering how important those pictures are."

"If it's any consolation the Gilded Lily is not a place any of your lady friends will frequent. There's no way any of them would know about the pictures. That is, unless their husbands told them."

"But there are other men from Dancing Deer, who might find out."

"Yes. That's true. And since your husband is on the city council, it might affect his political career."

"I could care less about that civic stint with his buddies. I wasn't planning on letting him run for another term anyway."

The screen door opened and one of Marianne's friends stuck her head outside. "We got a call from Betts. She's not sending the car till this evening. They varnished the stairs and it needs time to dry. We're getting a card game going. Why don't the two of you join us?" She looked at each of the two women, then closed the screen door and left.

Ophelia's spirits brightened with the stay of execution and said, "I love to play cards. Do they play for money?"

"Yes, but the stakes are small. The most I've ever lost was twenty dollars and the most I've ever won was a hundred. But they play like it's all the money in the world."

"Bridge?"

"No, poker. Several versions. Dealer's choice."

"I think I'll join them. It'll get my mind off what I got to do."

"Okay. We'll finish the make-up later. You look almost good enough like you are. That wig took off a few years and probably a few inhibitions."

Ophelia walked inside and took a seat at the kitchen table. Two other ladies were already settled.

"Hello, my name's Jennifer and this is Cassie. You must be new."

"Yeah. I'm a friend of Marianne's. My name is Minta."

"Pleased to meet you. You don't look like you're from these parts. You a foreigner?"

"My parents immigrated from Egypt before I was born."

"Wow, how'd you get into the business?"

"Just luck I guess. Do you have chips for keeping score?"

"No. We use bobby pins. A dollar each. I ran away from an abusive husband and Cassie here was a mail-ordered bride. She came all the way from Chicago. The man she had been writing turned out to be a pig farmer who didn't know what a bar of soap looked like. He's now found her and is a regular customer."

A third lady walked up. "My husband came home one night and announced he'd lost me in a game of cards. So what's your story, honey?"

Ophelia thought for a moment. "My family raised sheep. I was the oldest with one sister and two brothers. I took care of a large flock, herding them from one pasture to another. Water was scarce and the only well served several families and their animals. By custom we watered the sheep in the morning and again late in the afternoon. One day when I was bringing my sheep to the well there was a stranger there. He was extremely good looking and asked if anyone knew my father. I fell in love with him on the spot. All I could manage to say was that I would take him to the man he was looking for after the sheep had been watered. For the next thirty minutes, he helped me. He said his mother and my father were related and he had a letter from his mother to give to my father. I worked and watched him from the corner of my eye. I couldn't take my eyes off him. That night my father had him eat with us. My sister was two years younger than me and she also took a shine to our visitor.

"During the next month he helped my father manage our farm. He was skilled in animal husbandry and more or less took over their care. My brothers were still too young and my sister didn't have the inclination. During that time my sister, Cleo, was constantly in his company. They grew very close. No one knew or cared about my feelings toward the man. After a month, my dad and the man brokered a deal where he would work for my father for seven years. In return, my father promised, after the seven years were up, he could marry Cleo. I was distraught. He should've been mine. I was the oldest. I found him first. During those seven years, I became a recluse. No other man would do. I worked with him in the fields and we became close friends but not romantically involved.

"When the seven years were up my father threw a big feast. Cleo was having second thoughts about the arrangement, and I was upset. I always thought somehow I'd prevail over my sister, so when my father came to me and said for me to go to the man's bed chamber instead of Cleo, I agreed. Cleo was relieved, as she was still immature.

"That evening, all the males got roaring drunk and my father performed the ceremony according to our custom. When my new husband came to me, he fell in the doorway and I had to undress him and carry him to bed. The next morning, he awoke in my arms. He became hysterical, yelling obscenities at my father for deceiving him. Later that day, they brokered another deal. My husband would work for my father for seven more years and then he would marry Cleo. Two wives, can you imagine?

"I spent those seven years being the best wife I could. I gave him two sons and took care of his every need. But when the second seven years were coming to a close, he talked of his love for Cleo and how happy he would be with her for his wife.

"I went to my father and told him I'd leave if he went through with the bargain. He told me if I wanted to leave, I could live with a family friend. He said he'd send my children after I had settled in. When I wrote him and asked for my two boys, he replied that he couldn't part with them as they were now too dear to him.

I felt like I was in prison. His friend kept me under a close watch and reported everything I did. So one night I ran away. I thought I'd find work and hire someone to steal my children for me. This is the only work I could find."

"Minta, that's the saddest story I've ever heard. How long ago was it?"

"Five years. Every time I go to bed with a man, I think about my husband and my two little boys and begin crying. I don't get much in the way of tips."

"Honey, is there anything we can do?"

"Just be a friend."

"Minta, you'll always have friends here. We have to stick together. Men are skunks."

Four hours later Marianne came into the kitchen as the cards were gathered and the pot scraped into Ophelia's large cache of bobby pins.

Ophelia took the cards and, with only her right hand, she divided them into two equal portions, then deftly placed the bottom half on top. She expertly shuffled three times and set them on her right. Cassie cut. After burning the top card, Ophelia started dealing each person three cards face down.

"Okay, girls. This is seven card stud, low in the hole wild, roll your own. Everybody in."

"Yeah. Pot's right."

Marianne walked over beside Ophelia. "Can you make this your last hand? We got to redo your make-up."

CHAPTER 21 – TRICKS OF THE TRADE
Wednesday evening, December 19, 1945

While they waited on the car, Marianne thought it prudent to give Ophelia some last minute instructions. "Honey, most men like their women sweet, innocent, and young. But a few like them mean. The women acting the mean parts intersperse their language with rough, coarse, and suggestive words. They act the part of a woman in total control. Sometimes they use whips and hand-cuffs. Usually, though, they're just mean-spirited and end up berating their clients. I don't know why the men like that sort of behavior. It wouldn't work with a woman. If you have a problem with a customer try and decide which way he likes his women and be the other. He'll leave you alone and look for someone more satisfying.

"Some men just want companionship. Betts makes them buy tokens just the same. If you find one of those he'll monopolize your time and not allow you to sneak off to Twinkie's room. We make the talkers give us a token for each hour of conversation.

"Don't let anyone touch you. They're not allowed to touch or see the merchandise before paying, and under no circumstances are they allowed to hurt you in any way. There is a whistle on a cord attached to each bedpost. One blow on that whistle and, in seconds, your room will be full of irate women. One will be carrying a gun. That'll be Betts. We had a better arrangement at the Painted Lady. Claude hooked up a panel of lights in his room. He put switches in each of our rooms; each switch wired to one of those lights. When a trick became troublesome, we flipped the switch. Claude was there pronto with a baseball bat. No one gave him any trouble.

"The men are only allowed in certain areas of the house. They can go onto the front porch if they want to smoke or get fresh air. I've heard Betts used to let them smoke in the house until a smoker caught the drapes on fire. The front room is the biggest, where most of the transactions are agreed to. The parlor is more intimate. There we have a piano and a phonograph. Usually, the men who go to the parlor have a favorite woman they've been seeing or have homed in on. They'll cozy up in a corner or on a small settee. Since there is music, there is also more privacy for the conversations taking place.

"In the dining room are *hors d'oeuvres* and beverages. We don't have a liquor license so the only beverages allowed are iced tea, sodas, and lemonade. Not many women stay in the dining room as the men are bad about dribbling their food and drinks on our dresses. You can spend all you make cleaning your clothes. The men come in but soon leave when they realize the women only come to get a bite to eat and then leave.

"There's no bathroom available for the men. They have to go outside. Sometimes we'll ask them to wash in the bathroom attached to each bedroom. There are no doors on the bathrooms and the toilet lid opens with a key so they don't do anything other than wash it off in the sink.

"Betts is pretty sharp. I'd keep my distance from her. Still, she has so many girls she doesn't know them all and with the way she handles the money she doesn't need to. The men buy their tokens when they enter, then give the girls a token each trip upstairs. About half the time they'll give an additional dollar or two if they think the woman they chose put forth enough effort. The next day each girl cashes in her tokens.

"The room opposite and the first room on either side of the second-floor landing and both sides of the hall are community bedrooms. I don't mean there is more than one bed in each room. What I mean is that it doesn't belong to anyone in particular. There's an 'Occupied' sign on the inside of the door. It'll be placed on the outside when the room's being used.

"The other bedrooms are for Betts' regular girls. No one other than the women assigned and their tricks are allowed in those rooms.

"Each room has a door on the hallway and two interior doors linking to adjacent bedrooms. The end bedrooms have one door on the hallway and only one interior door. Twinkie's room is on the end.

"If Saucy knocks on the door, you got to hide in a hurry. There'll be no time to exit through the hall door. If there's no one in the next bedroom over, that might be the best place to go. But then again, a girl might be heading that way right then. It's a crapshoot, Ophelia. The closets are usually too full of clothes for a body to fit. Although I don't know for sure about the one in Twinkie's room. The first thing you ought to do is decide where you'll hide if you need to.

"Do you have any questions?"

"No. But I'm seriously thinking of chickening out."

CHAPTER 22 – HOOKERS, JOHNS, AND A MADAM

Wednesday evening, December 19, 1945

When the car arrived, six women crowded in. The driver was a little vexed. "Where'd we get the extra woman?"

"What's the matter? We thought you liked chauffeuring around beautiful women."

"I do. But yesterday, we had five and today we got six."

"Were you unemployed before you started driving us around?"

"Yeah."

"Would you like to be unemployed again?"

"Uh . . . no."

"Then we'll put up with no more complaining."

The driver pushed in on the clutch, "Miss Cassie, would you shift please?"

Cassie grabbed the gear shift knob between her legs and pushed up, over, and farther up."

Jennifer and Marianne walked beside Ophelia on the wet walkway behind the house to the kitchen door. Linda and Naomi followed with Cassie bringing up the rear. When they entered the kitchen, a cook was busy preparing small tidbits of food on large silver trays. Cassie picked up a glass of iced tea and followed the other women down the hallway, past the stairs, and through the wide opening into the front room.

There were already six men in various locations. Six women attended the men. Ophelia looked around the room to see if there might be somebody she knew or somebody who might know her. No one. And what's more, Betts wasn't there. She eased over to the door linking the front room to the parlor. If Betts came into the front room, Ophelia thought she'd step into the parlor, and if Betts came into the parlor she'd step into the front room.

"Hey, babe. You need someone to talk to?"

"No. I'm an undercover cop. Got a suspect under surveillance—can't party right now."

"Whoa. Who you watching?"

"Can't say. Can't leave my post either, not until I get relieved."

"Damn, this is exciting. May I help?"

"Hell, no. You want to jeopardize the entire operation?"

"No. Just give a thumbs up when you get relieved."

"Will do."

Saucy came over to Ophelia. "You got rid of him pretty fast."

"Yeah. He just wanted to talk."

"We're supposed to get a fraternity from Russellville by ten. You need to be gone by then. They can be rowdy and I don't think we're talented enough to keep you from being hauled off by a horny young man with money to burn."

"If I haven't got the pictures by then, I'll leave out the back anyway."

"Honey, your girlfriends are in a blue coupe at the end of the parking lot. As soon as you've got the pictures, go onto the front porch for fresh air. If there's no one there, you can run to the car and we'll cover for you. If there is somebody on the porch, you'll either have to wait for them to go inside or you can leave through the kitchen and make a sweeping circle, coming at the car from behind. You might want to check the location of the car so you'll know which direction you have to run and how far."

As the two women made their way to the front porch, Twinkie stepped off the staircase. The two ladies made a left turn in the foyer and headed up the stairs.

"Remember to hide if I knock."

Inside the bedroom, a small light gave a soft glow from a bedside nightstand. Obviously, Twinkie didn't want to be alone in the dark with a man she didn't know and probably didn't trust. Her job was not one Ophelia wanted. She looked around the room for a place to hide. She tried the door to the adjacent bedroom. It wasn't locked. None of the doors locked. No reason to lock out your rescue if you needed it.

Ophelia decided to check the closet first. There were boxes in the top, clothes hanging, and clothes piled on top of shoes on the floor. It didn't look like Twinkie could get another dress in and still shut the door. Ophelia pulled down a box. It held a hat. All the boxes had hats. Nothing in the pockets of the clothes. Nothing on the floor with the flung clothes laying atop the shoes. Ophelia stepped back, trying to decide where to look next. There was a knock on the door. She ran to the bathroom. No place in there other than behind a sheer shower curtain. Out from the bathroom she ran around the bed, opened the door, and stepped into a dark bedroom. Thank God no one was using it. Ophelia leaned her head against the door.

Twinkie's hall door opened. Ophelia could hear muffled talk. The bed creaked as if someone sat on it. She heard more muffled conversation, a zipper unfastened, the swoosh of clothes thrown and more creaking of the bed.

Ophelia's eyes finally adjusted to the limited light in her hiding bedroom. She looked around. It was just like the one she'd run from except reversed and with an additional door.

Ophelia put her head to the linking door. Only about ten minutes passed before the bed quit squeaking. She heard bits and pieces of conversation, then the hall door open and shut. That was a fast five dollars. She waited another minute and opened the bedroom door. Tiptoeing inside, she went straight to the nightstand. Ophelia needed to find the pictures and negatives and get the hell out of Sodom and Gomorrah. From the bathroom, someone turned on a water faucet. Ophelia froze.

There was a knock on the door. Ophelia dropped to the floor and rolled under the bed. Thank goodness for throw rugs. Twinkie came out of the bathroom and let in two people. Ophelia had counted the number of feet from under the bed.

"I thought you said you were going after Linda."

"This is Rosalinda. She's close enough."

"Think you can handle two women in the same bed?"

"Sure. Might solve my problem."

Rosalinda said, "Honey, what problem you got?"

"It's his lymphatic system." said Twinkie.

"His what?"

"His lymphatic system. He's emphatic about being limp."

"Oh, honey, Rosalinda will take care of that. But you got to wash first."

Ophelia surveyed her surroundings. Did she have enough clearance? Would the bed break from the gyrations of three participants in a group activity? Would a slat shatter and send a jagged piece through her heart? What would the police say when they found the wife of Dancing Deer's town pharmacist under a prostitute's bed? What would her family think? How long would she be there before someone pulled her cold body out from under the bed? Would they be looking for the cause of a foul odor? Ophelia shuddered.

She heard the thud of shoes hitting the floor, the jangle of change, and felt the bed sag when someone sat down.

"Oh, my God. I've dropped it." Someone entered from the bathroom. "Please be careful. Don't step on it."

"You go in there right now and wash it off. I don't want to touch nothing that's been dragged around on the floor and stepped on."

"It's my watch, Rosalinda. I dropped my watch."

Ophelia knew that when he got on his hands and knees to look for the watch she'd be found. Why did she have to have those damned pictures?

"Whew. Here it is. Can I put my pants on this chair?"

Ophelia thought the voice was vaguely familiar. It wasn't one of the boys. Oh, come on, let's get this over with.

"Okay, ladies. Can you get a handle on this?"

"It's got a handle?"

Twinkie started laughing. "No, Rosalinda, that's only a figure of speech."

Ophelia moved to the edge of the bed—as far from the activity as she could get. Then she saw it. A yellow envelope stuck in the bed springs. She quietly removed the envelope and unfastened the clasp. It was too dark to see what was inside so she reached in with her hand and felt the glossy slickness of the pictures. She counted to make sure all six were there, then reached to the bottom of the envelope to feel for the thin strips of negatives. They were there as well. From under her dress Ophelia pulled the envelope Claude had given her. She switched the good pictures with the ones already faded to nothing and traded the negatives with the ones Claude had supplied that were now too dark to print. She fastened the clasp and stuffed the yellow envelope back into the bed springs. She folded her envelope, with the good pictures and negatives, into a smaller size and stuffed it into her voluminous dress. Now all she had to do was wait for Rosalinda and Twinkie to finish their task.

"Ugh, your turn. I'm not making any progress."

More bed clanging. The pace quickened.

Fifteen minutes. It's lasted at least fifteen minutes. How long will this keep up?

Twinkie said, "Whew, I give up. I'm going for reinforcements. I need two more tokens. Anyone in particular?"

With a weary note, Ophelia heard an old man say, "There's a real pretty brunette I didn't see earlier."

"I know the one you're talking about. I'll find her. Rosalinda, you keep him happy. I'll bring the cavalry." The bed creaked as the participants altered positions. "Soon, sweetheart, you'll be covered in naked women."

Two women and three men sat in wicker chairs on the front porch. It was windy and cold, but the show was worth the effort. "Okay, the door's opening again. See, there's a man in goggles and painter's hat. Here comes a woman . . . and another woman. That's it. Now see, the last woman heads into the woods and the first two out of the car wait for the her return. Oops, there goes the man after her. In a minute they'll come back walking slower than when they left and everybody will get into the car."

"What's going on?" asked another person joining the group.

"Hard to say. There's a dark coupe at the back of the parking lot with a lot of activity going on in it."

"I'll say. All told, we think there are two motorcycling painters and three women involved. It's quiet for a while, then the car starts bouncing around like it's on springs, the car door opens, and several people get out, with one or two running to the woods. In a minute, they come back and get back into the car."

Another spectator said, "Both men are wearing goggles and painters hats. Sometimes both men go into the woods and sometimes two women. Then, at other times, it's a man and a woman."

"Well, men sometimes want to relive their high school days. You know, sex in the back seat sort of thing. These girls always try to please. If they're shown enough money, some of them will do anything."

"And the ones heading to the woods?"

"Giving the ones not going a little privacy."

"Okay, here they are back." The door opens and everyone crawls in.

Stacy Jo arrived around eight p.m. She walked inside like she owned the place. After surveying the front room, she walked toward the parlor when a man stepped in front.

"May I bring you an iced tea or lemonade?"

"No, thanks. I'm only going to be here a few minutes."

"You're not one of Betts' girls?"

"Heavens, no. I'm looking for my snake-in-the-grass boyfriend."

"If you find him and decide he's not worth salvaging, I know where you can make a sizable amount of spending loot."

"Doing what?"

"Just being nice to men like me. I'll pay a big bonus to be your first customer."

"No, thanks."

Stacy Jo walked away from the man to get a closer look at a woman now facing the wall.

"Miss Ryan, is that you?"

The woman slowly turned toward Stacy Jo. "Hello, Stacy. I understand you're working at a bank."

"Yes, I am. Miss Ryan, what are you doing here? This is the Gilded Lily, for God's sakes."

"Stacy, why don't we go into the dining room where we can talk?"

The two women soon sat in a back corner, their chairs pulled close together. "After my mother died, my father got sick and used his life's savings and everything I had put away to pay for his doctor and hospital stay. When we ran out of money, they said there was nothing more they could do and sent him home. On my salary from the school district, I didn't make enough to pay my bills and help out, so I started working here on weekends. With the additional money, I was able to pay for his medication. At least he didn't suffer any pain.

"My boyfriend found out and broke our engagement. I thought the world had come to an end. Then one Saturday the school superintendent came in and recognized me. He told me I could quit or he'd fire me."

"Why didn't you offer a compromise? By you keeping quiet about him frequenting this place, he might save his job. A threat to call the local newspaper should have been sufficient." Stacy put her arm around her favorite teacher.

"Honey, that sort of thing is played by a double standard. Men's immoral actions are tolerated where women's are not. I quit so that I could get another teaching job later in life. Right now, I'm earning three times what I received as a teacher. When I can't make that kind of money with my looks, I'll move somewhere and start teaching again."

"How much do you make?"

"I get five dollars per gentleman. On a good night, with tips, I can make thirty-five. Tonight, there's a bus coming in from Russellville and I might make fifty."

"In one night?"

"Yeah."

"Bob, did Clarice make it back?"

"No. She hasn't called and no one's here to fix my supper."

Johnston said, "No one's had any supper. I got worried about Betty and called Claude. Got no answer."

"We think they ran into some sort of problem finishing the stairs. Jump in. We're going to the Gilded Lily and see what's up." Rube opened his car door for Mayor Bob. "Scoot over, George, give Robert some room."

Twenty minutes later they pulled into the parking lot of the Gilded Lily and went all the way to the back for a parking space. They pulled right in front of a blue coupe that bore a striking resemblance to the one driven by Rube Abernathy's wife, Suzanne. The men paid little attention to the similarity, or to the five pair of eyes peering over the dash and from beside the front seat backs. Six men rushed into the most notorious establishment in northern Arkansas, while five women sat in a blue coup with smoke coming out of their ears.

Inside, the men went straight to the staircase to see if the women were still working. They stood in awe of the finished work, then separated like a swarm of mosquitoes at a nudist convention to see if the women might still be there. Faisal and Bob headed to the dining room where there would be food—albeit in small portions. They started with napkins and small plates then loaded the plates down until they started bending under the stress.

"Come on. Let's set these down and get something to drink. A couple of plates like these and the women can stay gone. I'll be good till tomorrow night."

"Shhh. Bob, there's Stacy Jo with her arm around the brunette."

"Where?"

"Right behind us and to the left, in the corner."

"Can you hear what they're saying? My hearing's not been so good since our run-in with the men from Skunk Hollow."

"I think they're talking about how much money a woman can earn here. The brunette says she can make fifty dollars per night."

"Good Lord. We need to put one of these houses in Dancing Deer."

"Let's get out of here before she sees us."

"Hey, fellas. I thought you'd head to where the food was."

Under his breath Mayor Bob said, "Shhh, Harold. Stacy Jo is going to work at the Gilded Lily. The brunette's telling her how much she'll be able to make."

"Hot damn. Stacy Jo looks just like my first love. They even have the same last name. Well, the same last name after my first true love left me and married another. Hell, I'm going over and offer to be a regular customer."

"Harold, if Boyd found out, he'd put you in the hospital. It'll be better if we tell him and you come see Stacy next week."

"Okay, I see your point. I can wait."

Stacy Jo and the brunette got up and walked toward the front room behind three men with their heads inches above their plates. The two women stopped at the stairs to admire Claude's work. Stacy Jo bumped into Twinkie when she backed up to get a better look.

"Twinkie, what are you doing here? Why are you wearing so much make-up?"

"Because, Stace, I work here. I wasn't as good a student as you. When I graduated, I had a hard time finding a job and didn't want to get married, so this was my only alternative. Besides, the men think I'm worth ten dollars for each trip upstairs."

Standing beside the stairs with Twinkie and Miss Ryan, Stacy was overwhelmed a third time when Ophelia descended the stairs. Stacy Jo took one step and stood directly in front of a blonde Ophelia Obadiah.

Back in the dining room, all six men from Dancing Deer were now devouring what remained of the food. Three were into their second plates. Not one of the six heard Stacy Jo yell, "Ophelia?"

Ophelia grabbed Stacy Jo's arm and headed to the porch. There were now ten people watching the dark coupe. Ophelia said, "Stacy Jo, I'll explain everything to you tomorrow." She then removed her heels, turned, and ran through the foyer with the staircase, past Twinkie and the brunette, down the hall, past the front room, past the parlor, and came to a screeching halt at the edge of the dining room. Faisal and five buddies were eating the food prepared for the johns. She did an about-face and ran back to the front of the house, opened the front door, zigzagged through the throng of onlookers, and used her hand to catapult over the railing into a flower bed.

Gathering up her skirt, Ophelia ran to the blue coupe. Its passenger door opened when she got within forty feet. At twenty feet, the engine started. The car was backing slowly from the parking space when Ophelia slid to a stop and jumped in. Before the door was completely shut, Suzanne started fish-tailing through the parking lot, she barely missed an arriving school bus of fraternity boys.

CHAPTER 23 – LLOYD'S ONGOING PROBLEM
Thursday morning, December 20, 1945

Stacy Jo emerged from the bathroom almost ready for work. She needed to change one more time. This was her morning routine. Usually, she changed clothes two or three times each morning. Either she couldn't remember when she had last worn a particular outfit, she got toothpaste on her collar, or the colors were not exactly right. It's a woman's prerogative to be finicky in her manner of dress, and Stacy Jo was a world champion.

Joyce waited for her. "Stacy Jo, he's already left. What time did you get in last night?"

"What are you talking about, Mother? I got home around nine."

"He must've thought you were staying with your girlfriend and left."

"Who was he? Mother, who was waiting on me?"

"Lloyd, dear."

"Lloyd?"

"Yes. He bought a Christmas tree and last night we got down the ornaments from the attic and decorated it." Stacy's mother walked over to the front window and plugged a cord into a wall outlet. Instantly, the room filled with the twinkling of red, blue, green, yellow, and white lights.

"It's beautiful. You decorated the tree with Lloyd? And he waited to talk with me? Did he say what it was about? Mom, are you sure it was Lloyd?"

"Yes, I think so. He didn't say why he was waiting, but he did tell me he loved you."

"Well, I don't love him. Mom, he's five years younger than me."

"It's only a number, dear."

"Yes, I know, but it's an important number."

"He didn't look like he was five years younger than you. I think he's a very nice young man, Stacy Jo. You should talk with him. He ended up staying Tuesday night waiting on you. I covered him with two blankets as he slept on the divan."

"Mom, I was here Tuesday night. I didn't see him on the divan."

"Yes, I know, dear. He must've been deep under the covers."

"Okay, I'll talk to him at work today. They've given him a new assignment and he doesn't finish until around lunch. They got him walking to the retail stores with Mr. Stanky, the security guard, picking up deposits."

"I like him, Stacy Jo. I don't care if he is younger than you."

That morning Stacy Jo tried to determine what she'd tell Lloyd. He was just a kid. He had a bright future, but he couldn't be thinking of a serious relationship with four years of college looming over his shoulder. Still, he had that silly look on his face. Probably the same look she'd had for her history teacher in the seventh grade.

At ten, he arrived with Mr. Stanky. They went straight to the cashier, who removed the briefcase from Edwin's wrist. Both men walked to the break area to warm before continuing to visit the merchants.

Stacy Jo pulled Lloyd aside, allowing Edwin to continue to the coffee pot by himself. "Lloyd, we need to talk."

"All day."

"All day?"

"It's just a figure of speech, Stacy. You can talk with me any time you want—all day, any day."

"Okay, I want it this day, right now."

"Let's go into my private office."

After opening his door, Lloyd pushed everything to one side and brought in a small folding chair from a conference room. "Have a seat, Stacy." He left his door ajar. He didn't want to get a rumor started. "I've been looking forward to actually talking with you. Stacy, I've got so much to say but maybe you should go first."

"No, you tell me what you have to say. It might make a difference in what I have to say."

"Stacy, you are so exciting. Every time I look at you my heart comes into my throat. I've never felt this way about a woman before."

"Lloyd, how many women do you know?"

"Uh, I don't know. There were several in high school. Then I came to Dancing Deer. There're lots more girls here. But that's no never mind. You're the prettiest by far."

"And you've been talking with my mother?"

"Yes. I thought you might like to have someone drive you to work. The streets are slippery when iced over."

"I can get myself to work, thank you. How old are you, Lloyd?"

"I don't see how age has anything to do with it. I'm old enough to work, to have a car, to make my way in the world. Don't you feel the same about me as I do about you?"

Stacy thought about using Lloyd to make Boyd jealous. However, Boyd had never done anything to make her jealous. He had made her mad, upset, and infuriated, but he had never made her jealous. Stacy needed a plan. Did Lloyd fit in the plan somewhere? Could he be brought into her confidence? Would he have any ideas to help her solve her problem?

Stacy stood from the chair. "Lloyd, thank you for the Christmas tree. It's beautiful and my mother thinks you're the sweetest man on earth, but I need to make myself perfectly clear on this. There is only one man for me and he is not you."

"But I thought . . ." Lloyd watched as Stacy turned and walked out of his office. "I thought you were a two-timing broad."

Boyd decided to go to the bank to see if Stacy might be working at her window. He'd plop down a deposit. No, better make that a transfer. He didn't have a deposit to make. And while she completed the paperwork, he'd apologize and set the gift in her change tray. It was a marvelous day to apologize. This was going to work out so well.

Boyd walked to her window. There was a placard saying 'Next Window' with an arrow pointing to his right. He looked down the hallway, past the vault, to Lloyd's office. There she was. He quickly walked to the next window, transacted his business, and walked away.

"Stacy, Boyd was just here."

"He was? Did he ask about me?"

"No. He transferred some funds and left. I think he came to see me."

When lunchtime approached, Mr. Jimmerson asked Stacy Jo if he could take her to lunch. Carla, Mr. Potter's personal secretary, and Jefferson Wiggins, the new accounts manager made it a foursome. They walked the few blocks to the Ritz Bistro. It had stopped snowing, but piles of snow had accumulated in drifts. Cody, the town wino, had made a basket-full of money cleaning the sidewalks in front of the merchant's shops. He'd be in booze till sometime in '46.

When they were seated, Stacy Jo looked around to see if Boyd might be there. He wasn't. She loved Boyd. She decided right then she'd go by his house after work and see if she could work her way into his heart again. Oh, no. What about the meal she'd left on the table? She'd have to clean it up, put things back as they were. Did she extinguish the candles?

Mr. Wiggins asked Mr. Jimmerson, "Charles, did you read Wednesday's paper?"

"No. We decorated our tree last night."

"They're closing the orphanage. The Catholic church is consolidating all the kids into a few of the bigger churches around the country. Charles, they're going to break up the children—brother from sister. I think it's cruel."

"I do too. Another injustice perpetrated against those poor children."

"Charles, you need to read the paper. Connie cried. The entire center section was written with articles on each child. Mr. Bell had pictures and stories. I think we're going to take some children into our home over the holidays and maybe adopt one for good."

"You and Constance don't have any children of your own?"

"No. Always wanted to but couldn't. Just think, we could have had one all along. I'm supposed to meet with Father O'Reilly after lunch. Do you think I could have an hour off?"

"Sure, Jefferson. Take the rest of the day. I'll cover for you. Are you going to adopt a girl or a boy?"

"I don't know. I'll leave that up to Connie."

Charles Jimmerson turned to Stacy Jo. "Sure sorry to see you leave, Miss Martin. I understand you want to be closer to your mother. Is she in poor health?"

"I'm not sure. She gets confused easily and can't remember things like she used to. My father died a few years ago and, if Mom stays busy, she seems to do okay. But if she sits or meditates, she gets depressed. She misses my dad. They had a happy marriage. I hope when I find my Mr. Right, he's as right for me as my father was for my mother."

Carla said, "That's a nice thing to say, Stacy. Are you looking for Mr. Right?"

"I think all single women are looking for Mr. Right. Sometimes we settle for Mr. Almost Right thinking we'll make adjustments."

"Kind of like a man who buys a new suit and has to have it altered to fit?" chimed in Jefferson.

"No. More like finding a pair of dungarees that need to be washed and patched before you can even try them on. And men are reluctant to change. They think they were good enough when you accepted their proposal and don't understand why you want to make alterations now."

"So, are you going to work at the bank in Skunk Hollow?"

"Yes. They offered me twenty-five cents less per hour and their building is not as bright and cheery as ours, but it's within walking distance of my house. I hope working through the New Year is an adequate notice."

"Oh, sure. Will you get a vacation? Any fringe benefits?"

"No."

"I'll keep your job open until February—in case you don't like it there—because we sure like you here."

"Thank you, Mr. Jimmerson. I think I'm going to cry."

The rest of the meal was taken up with small talk and, when they finished, they walked back to the bank, with Mr. Wiggins cutting across frozen grass to his car.

CHAPTER 24 – OPHELIA GOES BONKERS
Thursday morning, December 20, 1945

"How was I to know someone took pictures? We were trying our best to keep our butts from being kicked. It was nasty business. There were fifteen of them and seven of us. Why did you feel it necessary to buy the pictures?"

"Because you were stark naked. It should have been as embarrassing to you as it was to me."

"It wasn't embarrassing to me. I was proud of the fact that we were able to overcome those lopsided odds. Of course, I didn't much care to spend the night in jail, but Boyd hid our identification and the two cars. So when we told the police we were all John Smiths, they couldn't prove otherwise. Anyway, that's how the Greeks fight."

"How do the Greeks fight?"

"Naked."

"Well, I don't want the other women having their own picture of my husband displaying a . . . uh . . . a large you know what . . . for all to see."

"After I got over the initial shock, I was quite resigned to it. You're probably the envy of any other woman who saw the picture."

"I am not."

"So now, what are you going to do with the pictures?"

"I'm going to destroy them. And you better not get yourself into another compromising situation like that. Next time I'll . . . I'll . . . there's no telling what I'll do."

"I shudder to think. A vindictive woman on the rampage. You're more embarrassing to me than those pictures."

Ophelia had all she could take. From left field she brought up an open hand and smacked Faisal's face. "You half pint of narcissistic perversion. Get out of my house."

Faisal had already figured it was time to leave. The slap was only the exclamation point at the end of the sentence. He'd go to Mayor Bob's.

When Faisal arrived, he knew something was not quite right. Mayor Bob's car had been backed out of his garage and Mayor Bob was sitting in it playing the radio. Faisal parked and walked over to his good buddy. Through the driver's side window Faisal said, "What's up, Robert?"

"Hello, Faisal. You know how difficult Clarice can be. This morning I went to breakfast before shaving. I was wearing an undershirt and pajama bottoms with my hair standing tall down the middle."

"Pretty much like you are right now."

"Yeah. Clarice laughed and the girls said I looked scary. I hid behind the paper. After the meal, Clarice told the girls not to worry with the dishes. She said I would be doing them from now on."

"Ha, ha. You're doing the dishes?"

"No, I am not. I stormed out and have been here, waiting for someone to come tell me I can come back in that the dishes are done."

"How long you been waiting?"

"Two hours. Faisal, do you reckon she knows about us going to the Gilded Lily last night?"

"I don't see how. Maybe we should drive over to George's house and see if he's also suffering from spousal abuse."

"Can I go to your house and take a shower first?"

"No. I've been kicked out. Maybe we should go to Boyd's. He doesn't have a woman laying down the law."

"Yeah, he's a lucky man."

CHAPTER 25 – BOYD AND THE ELVES
Thursday morning, December 20, 1945

Faisal and Mayor Bob pulled into Boyd's circular driveway. Bob said, "Think he's home?"

"I see smoke coming from the chimney."

Boyd pulled up just as Mayor Bob and Faisal were walking to his front door. They waited. "What's going on, fellas? Bob, you look like you just got up."

"We've been kicked out. Can I use your bathroom to shower and shave? Where you been?"

"Had some bank business." Boyd reached into his pocket to make sure he still had the present he'd planned on giving Stacy Jo. "Are either of you going to work today?"

"No. We're taking the day off. I didn't have anything going on anyway."

"Yeah, me either," said Faisal.

"Is the fact that both of you got kicked out on the same day of any significance?"

"We don't know. Have you had any problems with Stacy Jo?" Faisal looked in the dining room. "Wow, look at your table. Plates of food, candles, an open bottle of wine. What's going on Boyd? You got a new woman?"

"No. Elves."

Mayor Bob and Faisal looked intently at Boyd while they waited for more.

"You guys remember the story of the shoe cobbler who was just making enough to feed his family? Then at Christmas, when he didn't have any money to buy presents, elves came while he slept and worked in his shop to make wonderful shoes."

"No," said Faisal.

"My grandfather read me that story when I was a kid," added Mayor Bob.

"Well, I think elves came and fixed me a meal of potatoes."

"Have you been praying for a meal of potatoes?"

"No, but, I've been dreaming about French fries."

"What about Stacy Jo? Could it have been her? Maybe she wanted to apologize for two-timing you with Lloyd."

"Or for three-timing you and Lloyd with that guy from Skunk Hollow."

"I thought about that. The food's cold. Had to have been done last night or maybe even the night before. I'm thinking it was Thelma."

"Johnston said Stacy was asking about you."

"Did he tell her about us talking with Lloyd?"

"No. He said he thought you were looking for her."

Boyd looked at his feet. "It's not the same without Stacy Jo around. I got to talk to her and get some things settled."

Mayor Bob started toward the bathroom. Over his shoulder he said, "Faisal, tell him about seeing Stacy Jo last night."

"Uh . . . Boyd, maybe you should sit down."

"You saw Stacy Jo last night?"

"Yeah. She's working at the Gilded Lily."

"She's what?"

"Now, Boyd. Don't get mad. Me and Bob didn't proposition her or anything. We went searching for the women. It was late and no one was getting fed. The women were supposed to help Claude finish and then come home. When they didn't show we thought it must be taking them longer than they expected. So, we went looking to see if we could help. They must've finished before we got there and passed us on the highway. When we arrived Stacy Jo was sitting in the dining room with her arms around the brunette. You know which one I'm talking about?"

"Yeah, I know the one."

"We loaded our plates and sat down to eat before we saw her. The brunette was telling Stacy how much money she'd be making. Me and Mayor Bob are thinking about opening our own place. We've already come up with a name. We're going to call it 'The Hoe-Downer.' Boyd, there were lots of men and a bevy of new girls at the Gilded Lily. Business is booming in the entertainment industry. Right before we left, an entire busload of college kids arrived. We'll make a fortune."

"Was she already working or just thinking about it?"

"We don't know. Mayor Bob had to stop Harold from transacting a deal right then. Boyd, you got to move on."

"Maybe we should talk with Betts. Tell her no one will come from Dancing Deer if she hires Stacy Jo."

"Boyd, if Stacy Jo starts working at the Gilded Lily, there will be a lot of men from Dancing Deer making their first trips to a whorehouse. Stacy Jo will be the most popular girl there."

Boyd lowered his head into his hands.

"We didn't see Betts but did get to see our finished handiwork. Damn good job. That staircase is now the focal point of the entire place—it and the girls. After we ate and decided our ladies weren't there, we left."

Boyd slumped in his chair. He didn't say anything just run his fingers in little circles on the armrest. Presently he said, "Her mother did say she had a new job in Skunk Hollow." Boyd sat back in his chair and looked out the window. "Faisal, I need a drink."

"Let's let Mayor Bob get a shower and we'll drive by some of the other guy's houses and see if any of them have been kicked out. Then we'll go to Snockered and tie on a few. The women are getting ridiculous. Ophelia called me a pervert. Can you imagine, me a pervert? I'm a druggist—a respected professional, for God's sakes."

Boyd got up from his chair and walked to the telephone. "Jenny, what're the guys working on? No, I won't be in today. Yeah, okay. Let them have whatever they want. She's got to have water. Be sure they wrap them this time. I'll try and come in tomorrow. Thanks, Jenny." Boyd hung up the telephone.

"It's no fun being a plumber in the winter: damn cold work; muddy, frozen pipes; clogged sewer systems. I sometimes think Dad hated me. He's probably looking down at me from heaven with a big grin on his face. He knew I didn't want his business."

"Boyd, you got the best plumbing company in Marsden County. And you got good employees. All you gotta do is sit back and let them make you money."

"And what about you, Faisal? Who counts the pills when you take off?"

"My brother. He's a hard worker. He loves to work about as much as I love to goof off. I paid for his schooling. I figure he's got another twenty years of working his shifts and covering half of mine to get back to even."

Mayor Bob came out of the bathroom. "Boyd, you got any clothes I can borrow?"

"Hell, no. You got forty pounds on me. Besides I haven't had time to replace everything Stacy Jo burned. If you can't go back home we'll have to go to, uh, let's see, Johnston is too tall and skinny, Harold— Harold's the right size."

Harold was spoon-feeding his mother-in-law on the glassed-in front porch Imogene now called the California room. "Come on, Mom. Just a few more bites. Imogene says you got to eat everything she put on the plate. You always liked carrots before, and green beans—there ain't nothing wrong with them." Harold laid the spoon of carrots down as his three buddies walked up.

"What's up, Harold? You playing nursemaid?"

"So succinct the statement; so true the tirade." Harold wiped drool from his mother-in-law's chin. "Imogene said . . . uh, boys, you ought to taste these carrots. Imogene seasoned them with caramelized brown sugar. They're to die for. Mother Lucille hasn't eaten a bite. Here, want a taste?"

"Imogene tell you, if you don't get Mother Lucille to eat it, you got to?"

"Yeah . . . but."

"No, thanks. We're headed to Snockered. Going to play a few games of pool and get wasted. We been kicked out of our homes."

"Boyd too. Who kicked Boyd out?"

"No, just me and Faisal. Harold, can I borrow a change of clothes? They won't let me in Snockered wearing pajama bottoms."

"You got to eat Mother Lucille's lunch."

"Damn, Harold. Ain't you got a dog?"

"No."

"Oh, all right. Give me that plate." Bob took a small bite of the carrots, gagged, and frantically looked for something to wash it down. Harold held out a glass of milk. Bob grabbed the milk and took a big swig. He gagged again. This time spitting what he hadn't swallowed into a hanging plant. "Damn, Harold, that was buttermilk. You need to tell someone you got diesel when they're expecting regular."

"I'll go get the clothes and a glass of water. You go ahead and eat the rest of the food. You're doing real good, Mayor Bob."

"Faisal, I'll pay you ten dollars to eat the rest of this food."

"Bob, you'd have to offer a hundred before I'd even entertain the idea."

"I'll eat it for twenty."

All three men looked at Mother Lucille. Boyd handed her the plate and spoon. She said, "Let's see the money. And someone needs to get me a clean spoon."

"Boyd, can I borrow twenty? I ain't got my billfold. Ain't even got a pocket to put a billfold in." Mayor Bob walked to the bathroom after taking a twenty from Boyd and handing the bill to a frail, small, and greedy hand.

Harold came out of his bedroom and handed over a pair of pants and a shirt to Faisal. "Here, you take him this and I'll get another spoon."

When Harold returned, he had a spoon and a glass of water. Boyd said, "Who's gonna watch her if we go to Snockered? Where's Imogene anyway?"

"Shopping with some of the other ladies." Harold sat on the swing next to Boyd and watched his mother-in-law guzzle the last of her food. "Maybe I could get the next-door neighbor."

"For another twenty, I'll take a nap."

CHAPTER 26 – SNOCKERED
Thursday noon, December 20, 1945

Boyd patted Faisal's back. "Stop for a minute, there's Lloyd walking with Edwin. I need to tell him something."

Boyd got out of the car and intercepted the two men as they marched from one retailer to another. "Good morning, fellas. Lloyd, could I talk with you for a minute?" Edwin gave them some space by sitting on a fire hydrant. Boyd continued loud enough for both to hear, "Lloyd, are you having any problems with Stacy."

"Yeah. She won't have anything to do with me. Could it be that guy in Skunk Hollow?"

"I don't think so. I've heard she's going to work at the Gilded Lily. I was hoping between the two of us we might talk her out of it."

"She gave her notice to Mr. Jimmerson, saying she was going to work at the bank in Skunk Hollow, making less money."

Boyd thought for a moment then said, "Damn, that means she's taking the job working weekends so she can still work at the bank. That way she won't have to tell her mother about the hooking job. Lloyd, what can we do?"

"Man, I don't know. Your name is Boyd, right?"

"Yeah."

"Boyd, she more or less told me to take a hike. She said I wasn't the man for her."

"Guess I'm not either. You're a handsome guy in that suit, Lloyd. Looks like she's changing quality for quantity."

"Boyd, if you can think of some way I can be of assistance without getting slapped, I'd be happy to help." Lloyd shifted his weight and then with a little more excitement in his voice asked. "How much you think she'll be charging?"

"The girls go for ten dollars. Sometimes their customers give them a dollar or two tip. You might want to check 'em out. There's one real pretty brunette. I think she's more your type. That damn Stacy Jo probably wouldn't put up with a man not having but a hand-full of experience.

"If you do go, walk lightly. I've heard rumors. Betts—she's the woman who runs the place—carries a gun. And then there's always the possibility of catching a venereal disease. No known cure. You develop boils all over your body so bad you can't bathe for fear of breaking one open. Then they start changing to a yellowish purple bubble of gelatinous flesh. It's not long after that till those boils start bursting open on their own. A yellow pus seeps out and stains the body so bad people start thinking you're oriental. No, when all those men in Skunk Hollow started vomiting blood, me and the boys had to quit going to the Gilded Lily."

Boyd walked back to Faisal's car, leaving Lloyd and Edwin with a ridiculous situation to ponder.

That night, Boyd, Harold, Faisal, and Mayor Bob sat astride barstools at Snockered. All had been drinking and were having a hard time staying upright on their seats. Of the four, only Boyd had danced. The last two times when the pace of the music changed his feet couldn't keep up with his legs and he'd fallen both times. Once he brought down the girl he was holding and the second, three members in a line dance. After that, he declined all offers.

"Okay, here's one:

'There was a young maid from Madrass
Who had a magnificent ass
Not rounded and pink
As you probably would think
But was gray, had long ears, and ate grass.'"

"Ha, ha. That's terrific, Harold. Now listen to this one:

'There was a young maid from Nantucket
Who kept her liquor in a bucket
Along came her beau
With her, wild oats he would sow
She said 'What the hell . . .'"

"Go on, Bob. What's the last line?"

"I don't remember. Damnit, I knew this was going to happen. When I have a few I can't remember squat."

"Okay, no more limericks for you."

"No more liquor either."

"What?" Mayor Bob turned around on his barstool and looked into the piercing black eyes of Deputy Sheriff Rafe, or maybe Ralph, Johnson.

"You heard me. No more drinks for you guys. You got someone I can call to take you home?"

"No. Our wives have kicked us out. We got no place to go."

"All of you?"

"Well, not Boyd. He's single. Ain't no one tells him what to do."

"Except the law," corrected Boyd.

"Okay, I'll call you a cab to take you to Boyd's. Sleeping it off at Boyd's is better than spending the night in the county jail."

"Yes, sir. Officer, how about one more drink while we wait?"

"Nope. Barkeep, bring these boys their tab."

CHAPTER 27 – GLADYS
Thursday early afternoon, December 20, 1945

Gladys had a problem to solve. She had to buy Edwin a Christmas present and had only four days to do it. And she had no money. She thought she'd take her problem to Father O'Reilly. He was such a smart man and so intuitive, he could see clear pictures through cloudy glass.

When she arrived, Jefferson and Constance Wiggins were leaving with two of the orphan girls. Connie ran to Gladys. "Gladys, I've got some people for you to meet. They're coming to visit for the holidays. I'm going to show them how to cook, but first we're going to buy a Christmas tree. How about you and Edwin coming over Saturday night? We can watch the girls decorate the tree, and then I'm going to show them how to make divinity.

"Gladys, this is Penny and this is Laurie. Girls, this is Mrs. Stanky."

"Hello, Gladys." Father O'Reilly held out his hand.

A few minutes later, Connie, her husband, and the two girls were gone and Gladys had been offered a seat in Father Donovan O'Reilly's study. Mrs. Holloway brought in a carafe of coffee and a plate of scones.

"How are you and Edwin doing?"

"We're wonderful Father. I want to thank you for your counseling. I couldn't be happier. But I've now got a problem. I haven't bought Edwin a Christmas present since our first year of marriage. He takes such good care of me and I feel like I've taken him for granted these last twenty years. I want to make it up to him this year but don't have any money. Can you give me an idea of how I can raise some money?"

"I understand the retailers are having a banner season. You could probably get a job working for one of them or you could sell something you no longer need. You don't have enough time to put it in the paper, but you could stick it on your driveway with a 'For Sale' sign."

"Father, you're wonderful. I think I now know what to do."

Minutes later, Gladys talked to Ava at Ava's Dresses. "I can help customers pick colors and styles that complement their appearance. I can wrap or clean—anything you need."

"Okay, Gladys, I can pay you an hourly salary plus a commission on the sale of some dresses and other items I'm trying to unload. You know—got to make room for the new. When can you start?"

The front door opened with Lloyd Garrison and Edwin striding through. "Gladys, here's your husband. He's come for my money. What a relief not having to walk to the bank carrying a day's receipts. They now come and get it." Ava waved to the men and went into her office, followed by Lloyd.

Gladys got up from her chair and kissed her husband on his cheek. "Hi, handsome. You fought off any bandits today?"

"Not yet. You shopping?"

"No. I'm going to work through Christmas Eve. They need someone to help."

"Gladys, what's got into you, girl?"

"Oh, nothing. Ava just needs some seasonal help."

"Okay." Edwin rested the briefcase on the edge of a chair. "Have you heard anything about the men in Skunk Hollow vomiting blood?"

"No. Is it contagious?"

"Not unless you're frequenting the Gilded Lily."

Ava came out of her office with Lloyd, who stuffed an envelope in the satchel attached to Edwin's wrist.

"Edwin, this was the last one. Let's go back to the bank."

After the men left, three customers came in, and Ava grabbed Gladys before she had made it out the front door. "How about starting now?"

CHAPTER 28 – AVA'S DRESSES
Thursday late afternoon, December 20, 1945

"Gladys, bring me this one in blue." Summer Satterfield had joined her friends in a shopping frenzy at Ava's Dresses. She passed Clarice coming out of the dressing room as she was going in. "Clarice, that one looks so right for you. Does it have extra buttons? If you have to replace one of those fancy buttons and the dress doesn't have an extra sewed on somewhere, you might have to replace them all."

When Ava told Gladys she would get commissions in addition to her hourly wage for unloading some old inventory, Gladys had dollar signs pop into her eyes. She called her girlfriends, talked Ava into reducing the price on the stale merchandise another ten percent, and she was off to the races.

"So tell me, Gladys, why are you working? You've never worked before." Suzanne fondled costume jewelry.

"I want to buy Edwin something special for Christmas and didn't want to borrow the money from him. It's just four days."

Suzanne was floored. "You're working so you can spend your hard-earned money on Edwin? Rube isn't getting a damn thing from me. He'll be lucky if I feed him. Gladys, the men have been stinkeroos. They don't deserve presents."

"Well, maybe some of the men have exhibited less than honorable morals, but Edwin hasn't done anything more than lose that bet to Bill. He deserves whatever I can get for him. I know for sure he'll be getting me something nice. Something more than I deserve. So what will Rube be getting you?"

"I don't know. I've left him numerous hints. There's a fabulous set of pearls at Creighton's Jewelers."

"So you're not getting him anything, but you want him to buy you an expensive set of pearls?"

"That's it."

"Are they earrings or a necklace?"

"Both. You know pearls come in different shades. You have to find the shade of pink that looks good with your complexion. They only have the one set and it just so happens that they go with my complexion perfectly. I've shown them to Rube twice. This morning I went by and they were gone. I think my husband is carrying them around in his pocket."

"Gladys, I need a larger size in this one. Do you have a hat that matches?"

"I'll see."

"Gladys, I've picked out three. You sure I'll get the discount?"

"Certainly, I'll ring it up myself."

"Wow, Gladys, where'd you learn so much about fashion?"

"I don't know. I just wear what Eddy says I look good in."

"Well, you're sure looking good right now. My John told me I should join you in your jogging. In fact, he begged me."

"Betty, you really should. I run the loop around town every morning."

"My God. How many miles is that?"

"Four."

"I can't run four miles. I can't run a city block."

"You could start off by riding a bicycle beside me. Just get started. The hardest part is to get started. I've lost twenty pounds and now don't have high blood pressure. Eddy says I'm so sexy he's getting razzed by his friends on the police force."

The door opened and in walked Stacy Jo. "Gladys, we got a sale going on?"

Ava walked over to Gladys. "Gladys, I've been putting your name on the sales tickets. I want you to get the credit for all these sales. It looks like today is going to be the store's biggest weekday ever."

"That's great, Ava." Gladys turned to Stacy Jo. "We're marking down the dresses on these three racks and we have two tables of accessories on sale. You know, Stacy, you ought to try a brighter shade of red lipstick. We've got a brand that's guaranteed not to smear and another that's guaranteed will smear, for when you're marking territory. Say you're telling everyone Boyd is off-limits, and then you'd use the second one.

Stacy Jo had tears in her eyes. "Gladys, I've lost Boyd."

CHAPTER 29 – HANDS IN THE AIR
Friday mid-morning, December 21, 1945

"Officer, I was walking down the sidewalk and I heard some commotion in the alley. I looked to see what was going on and saw a man holding a briefcase and two others chained to a fire escape."

"Did you recognize the man with the briefcase?"

"No, sir. First time I ever saw him."

"Go on."

"One of the chained men was Edwin Stanky. He yelled, 'I know you. I'll come after you if it takes the rest of my life.' That's when the man with the briefcase shot him. It was terrible. Edwin couldn't even fall to the ground. He was handcuffed to that other fella. Their hands were high over their heads and linked together through the fire escape."

"What did the man with the briefcase do?"

"He walked out of the alley past me, got into a black Ford, and drove west."

"Did you get a look at his face?"

"Sort of. He had his hat pulled down to his nose."

"What about the license plate on the car?"

"I thought about that. There wasn't one. Is Edwin going to be all right? He comes past my house twice a day. I always felt safe knowing he was watching things for me."

"I don't know. He was unconscious when they loaded him in the ambulance."

"Do you want me to call Gladys? She's a good friend of my wife's."

"No. We'll take care of that. He's one of ours. But we'll need for you to go in a squad car to headquarters and make a written statement. We also got some mug shots for you to look through."

"Glad to be of help."

Another officer walked up as the witness was led away. "Sir, we found a single forty-five shell casing. He must've been using an automatic. We also have some broken links where he cut the chain tying the briefcase to Edwin's wrist."

"He didn't throw down the bolt cutter?"

"No, sir. Must've taken it with him."

"I guess we've got a seasoned veteran here. Put an APB on a black Ford heading west on Highway twenty-one. Maybe, we'll get lucky."

Chief of Police Steve Trent got into his squad car and headed to Edwin Stanky's house. This was not going to be easy. After a few knocks, he decided Gladys wasn't home.

Gladys found out when a hysterical woman charged in from the street saying a police officer was hanging from a fire escape two blocks over. Gladys grabbed her purse and flew out the door. She was there moments after the ambulance had left. She took off her heels and, holding her dress and swinging her purse, ran the fourteen blocks to the hospital. The emergency room nurse pointed the direction Edwin had been wheeled on the gurney. Gladys went down the hall as far as she could, stopping in front of a sign that said, "No Admittance." Frustrated and nearly overcome with fear, she ran to the admitting desk.

"Honey, they're giving him blood. I understand Doctor Rayne is going to probe for the bullet. Edwin's pretty bad. You go into the waiting room and I'll see what else I can learn."

"Please, Lord, don't let him die." Gladys took a handkerchief from her purse and blew her nose. Her system was overloaded with panic. He had been the good husband; she the bad wife. Always nagging, he'd never lived up to her expectations. Just lately, she'd come to realize how wrong she'd been. Edwin was the perfect husband and she hadn't had time to show him how her attitude had changed, how much she loved him.

The admitting clerk led her to the waiting room. One other couple waited for news of their sick baby. Gladys fell into an overstuffed chair still holding the arm of the clerk. "Honey, I'll be right back," the clerk said.

It seemed like an eternity before the woman came back. "Gladys, he hasn't regained consciousness yet. They've stopped the bleeding and are prepping him for surgery. I'll let you know what's happening as I find out."

Fifteen minutes later, Stacy Jo came over from the bank. "Oh, Gladys, I'm so sorry. Edwin was always nice to me. I can't believe this could happen in our little town."

"Thank you, Stacy. I think there's crime everywhere—even in Dancing Deer."

"Do you know anything yet?"

"Just that they've stopped the bleeding and they're getting ready to go after the bullet. I don't even know where he was shot. I won't be able to take it if he dies. I love him so much. Stacy, life's short, you got to make the most of it while you can. I haven't told Edwin I love him for a long time. I'm ashamed of the years when I wasn't good to him. Oh, Stacy, what if he dies? What'll I do?"

"Gladys, I'm here for you. We're all here."

At that moment, Suzanne Abernathy, Clarice Springer, and Summer Satterfield walked up. Summer handed Gladys a fresh handkerchief. "Is there any word?"

Gladys shook her head and dabbed at her eyes. The five women pulled up chairs, making a tight circle. Betty Baker and Imogene Greenleaf came in to join the group. Several low conversations started as information slowly saturated the area.

When Ophelia arrived, Stacy Jo jumped up and intercepted her fifteen feet short of the rest of the women. "Ophelia, you're living life in the fast lane. What possessed you to . . . to . . . do they know?"

"Of course they know. They're as guilty as me. Except for Gladys, they're all a party to it. Stacy Jo, we need to keep this to ourselves. Promise me you won't say anything."

"I won't say anything, but I think you're making a big mistake. Twinkie says they're ten dollars each. Seems a little low for the risk you have to take and the stigma attached."

"Maybe the first ones are ten dollars each. They'll go up from there depending on demand. If I didn't think it was worth it, I wouldn't have tried."

"Judging from what I saw last night, demand's pretty high."

"You've seen?"

"Yeah and I am shocked by your participation in such an outrageous situation. The brunette the men have been talking about was one of my high school teachers. And Twinkie, the tall one in pink—we shared a locker."

The two women stopped their discussion when they reached the group now discussing where the men were. Imogene said Harold hadn't come home from the night before. She said Mother Lucille confided to her that he'd left with three other men.

Ophelia jumped in to offer her opinion. "Faisal's missing as well. I got mad and threw him out of the house. I didn't think he'd stay gone all night. I guess he's one of the three men with Harold."

"Robert left in his pajamas. I didn't think he'd go far the way he was dressed. And he hadn't showered or shaved. I was wrong. I drove to the Gilded Lily and parked in the trees. None of our guys were there last night. So Bob was probably one of the three men, and I don't know where they went or where he is right now.

Stacy Jo said, "Gladys, I have to get back to the bank. I'm on my lunch hour. If I get to talk with Lloyd, I'll find out what happened and get back to you. Will you be here?"

Gladys nodded. She pursed her thin lips together and gave Stacy a grim smile.

CHAPTER 30 – JESSE'S PAPER
Friday afternoon, December 21, 1945

"I want everybody on it. Find out where he came from, what his name is, what color his socks are. I want to know what makes this man tick. We'll call in all favors. Stay out of the way of the police. Check in every hour and report what you've found. We'll be piecing the data together at command central and writing the story for tomorrow's paper.

"I want someone to interview this Lloyd character. I want someone to interview Charles Jimmerson, the witness interviewed by the police, and the owner of the last stop they made. See if the police want to make a statement. Talk to the concierge at the Ritz, the maids who made up his room, the waitresses who served him his meals, and to Big John Lynch, where he got his gasoline. If you run across someone on the list, but he's not your assignment call Mitzi. Either the original assignee will be contacted and he'll be heading your direction or the interview will be added to your assignment and deleted from the original assignee. Check out a camera. Let's get some pictures, people.

"Deadline is nine o'clock. From then until midnight, we'll all work to get the stories ready to be typeset. By four a.m. I want everything handed to Ivan for printing. Any questions?"

"Yeah. Who's doing what?"

"Look at the board. Mitzi put everything I just said on the board and right now she's putting names to go with the assignments." Jesse paused while his reporters, secretaries, the receptionist, and even Ivan ran to see if their names were written beside anything.

"Remember to check in every hour. New assignments will be given out as soon as you finish the one you're on. Okay, everyone, let's roll."

The *Marsden County Meteor* was reeling. Last week it gave most of its space to the children at the orphanage. From Wednesday morning until noon on Friday, they were deluged with telephone calls. It seemed like everyone in Dancing Deer wanted to open their home to an orphan for the holidays. Most of the phone calls went like the last one. "How do I go about getting one of them orphans to come celebrate Christmas with me?"

Then, at noon, word came down that Edwin Stanky and a new kid from the bank had been robbed picking up deposits from the retailers, with Edwin taking a bullet to the chest.

"Mitzi, bring me a camera. I'm heading to the hospital to interview Edwin's doctor—and anyone else I can find."

Jesse hung his camera from a strap over his shoulder and hid it, more or less, under his arm. He walked into the hospital and went straight to the admitting clerk. "Is there any information you can give me about Mr. Stanky?"

"Mr. Bell, all I can tell you is that Doctor Rayne stopped the bleeding and removed the bullet from his chest. He's still in Intensive Care with a nurse monitoring his condition. I've heard the doctor said he was in good physical condition with a strong heart. Still, I think everyone's worried. His heart stopped at one point. It took two minutes of massaging to get it going again."

"Can I use any of that in the paper?"

"Talk to Doctor Rayne first. I'll see if the Hospital Administrator has any objection."

Jesse walked down the hall to the waiting room. Several people had gathered around Gladys, who was lost in the confines of a large chair. The people parted to let Jesse in to give his sympathy.

"Gladys, I'm so sorry for Edwin. I understand he's a real hero."

"Yes, but he was my hero long before he stood up to that hoodlum."

"Have they given you any word on his condition?"

"Only that Doctor Rayne was successful in removing the bullet. Edwin's in Intensive Care right now. Someone's supposed to come and get me when he's stabilized."

Father Donovan O'Reilly laid his hand on Jesse's arm. "Be careful, Jesse. Gladys has been crying so much the floor is slippery with tears."

"Gladys, do you have anything to say to the readers of the newspaper?"

"Oh, I don't know. I would like them to pray for him. And to speak up if they know anything about the man who shot him."

"You look so pretty. May I take your picture to use with that request?"

"Jesse, I don't look pretty. My hair's a mess, my makeup's gone, my dress is wrinkled, and I've got mud up to my kneecaps."

"You look pretty to me and the readers will understand. You should look a little disheveled after what you've been through. Besides, I'm going to ask the bank to open an account for those who want to help you pay the medical bills."

"Mr. Jimmerson said the bank would pay everything. They're even going to continue his salary while he convalesces."

"Yes, Virginia. There is a Santa Claus."

CHAPTER 31 – FATHER O'REILLY'S DILEMMA
Friday afternoon, December 21, 1945

Jesse left Gladys to find Doctor Rayne, but, before he had gone very far, Father Donovan O'Reilly caught up and asked for a moment of his time.

"Sure, Father. You surprised by the response you've received from last Wednesday's paper?"

"Yes. That's what I want to talk to you about. Jesse, we've received numerous telephone calls asking if the children would like to spend the holidays with Dancing Deer families. Some are talking about actually adopting."

"I think that's great."

"I also did, at first. But the children want to celebrate Christmas with each other. They're just one big family. Anyway, I suggested that we get together at the church on Christmas Eve so the children can exchange presents among themselves. To the families, I suggested they supply whatever was needed to let their new charges make their presents. The children don't have money of their own, but they're all hard workers."

"That's wonderful, Father. May I interview some of the families and take their pictures for next week's paper?"

"Sure. But what I really want is for some families to make the same offers to the boys. All ten of the girls are visiting but only one of the boys. He's Andy, the youngest at five. The remaining boys range from seven for Lacy, who's now walking on crutches, to Terrell, who's fourteen."

"It must be the women who've decided to invite someone into their homes and the women prefer one of their own gender."

"Yes. That's the way I see it. I know this robbery is dreadful and you will most likely devote most of tomorrow's paper to it." Father O'Reilly looked Jesse through his eyes straight to the depths of his soul.

"Do you think you could devote a small section to the plight of the boys?"

"I certainly will. Thank you, Father, for bringing this to my attention." Jesse took out his memo pad and hastily wrote something. "Did the families agree to come to the church for Christmas Eve?"

"Yes, but we're celebrating at the Ritz. Bill Potter's back and suggested we have the get-together in the largest of his conference rooms. He's going to supply everyone with free food. I don't know what's come over Bill these last few months. He's finally filled with Christmas spirit."

"I'd like to take some pictures."

"That would be wonderful. Would you like to talk to Doctor Rayne? He never turns down the church, even though, he never attends."

"I'll just hang onto your frock."

CHAPTER 32 – A MEAL WITH LLOYD
Friday afternoon, December 21, 1945

"Lloyd, can we talk?"

"Stacy, I'm getting my things and leaving for the day. My nerves are shot. My hand is so jittery I can't draw a straight line—much less add a column of figures."

"I thought they gave you a new comptometer."

"They did, but I'm still taking the rest of the day off. You're welcome to talk to me while I get my stuff."

"Lloyd, I told Gladys I'd find out what happened."

"Very commendable. How about you and I eating at the bistro and I'll tell you everything."

"All right."

"But you've got to tell me everything as well."

"About what?"

"The Gilded Lily for one thing."

"You know about that?"

"Me and Boyd had a long talk. He was the one who suggested I talk to you in the first place."

"Boyd?"

"Yeah, and we both want to know about the guy in Skunk Hollow."

Stacy Jo was beside herself. Lloyd and Boyd were not friends, were they? What's going on? How did they know about her trip to the Gilded Lily? Who's this guy in Skunk Hollow? She needed to get to the bottom of this.

The rest of the day Stacy Jo pondered her situation. She planned, adjusted, revised, and aborted every strategy she could come up with. She needed more information. You can't make proper decisions while fumbling in the dark.

At three she closed her teller's window and started to balance her drawer. It was hard to do. She couldn't stay focused and ended up counting her bills five times before coming up with the same number twice. The change was even harder. Thelma had finished long before Stacy. Then Stacy Jo had to tally the checks, the withdrawals, the transfers, the loan payments, the certified checks, the cashier's checks, and the money orders. It was a nightmare getting everything sorted, calculated, and balanced against the paperwork. At five-fifteen, she stumbled out the front door, exhausted.

By five-thirty, she had parked her car and ushered by the *maître d'* to a prominent table in the center of the dining area where Lloyd was looking over the wine list. "They'll not let you order anything out of that book. You've got to be twenty-one to order anything with alcohol in it."

"I think today they'd consider it. I've had two offers to pay for my meal, several doors opened, and a valet parked my car for free."

"Celebrity status?"

"Yes, ma'am."

"Okay, Lloyd. Tell me what happened."

"I've already told the police. Do you mind if we order first?" Lloyd looked at Stacy. She pursed her lips together and let one corner of her mouth slide up a bit. He continued with, "Do you know what escargot is? Someone told me I haven't eaten until I've tried the escargot."

"No. Don't have any idea. This is not a restaurant I can frequent very often. The food's too rich and I'm too poor."

"You should have that under control shortly."

The waiter walked up and asked if they would like to order.

"Do you have escargot?"

"Certainly. As an appetizer, sir?"

"Yes. Is an order enough for two?"

"Oh, yes, sir. And one of our most popular dishes."

"Very well. And a glass of your house red wine, a cabernet."

The waiter looked at Lloyd with one eye closed and the other a little squinted.

"It's for me. I told him I wanted the wine. Here's my driver's license. And he'll take an iced tea—unsweetened. We'll order the entrees in a minute or two."

"Very well, Miss. But you'll have to join our Cocktail Club."

After the waiter left, Stacy Jo looked intently at Lloyd. "Well, that could've gone better."

"If you had left well enough alone, I could have persuaded him to bring me that wine."

"Lloyd, how old are you anyway?"

"Nineteen."

"When you go to college will you pledge with one of the fraternities?"

"I don't know. Hadn't thought about it."

"If you do, you'll get all the liquor you can handle. I've heard my girlfriends talk about the fraternity parties they've been to. You'll be in for some wild times."

"Do they ever go to the Gilded Lily?"

"A bus from Russellville was there last night."

"And how do you know that?"

"Just something I heard at the water cooler. You know how gossip goes around. But, maybe you don't. Do the men talk about such things?"

"Not the men I hang around with."

The waiter appeared with a shallow bowl covered with a silver dome. He placed a glass of iced tea in front of Lloyd and a stem of wine in front of Stacy Jo. A long slender tray of garlic bread wrapped in a slick and pliant gingham fabric was placed beside the table candle. And in front of each person, the waiter placed a small dish with a tiny fork. On a slender pad of paper he wrote the remainder of their order and left.

Lloyd raised the lid. His olfactory senses were overwhelmed with the rich aromatic smell of melted butter, garlic, and other spices he didn't recognize. "I don't think we should eat the shells. What do you think the forks are for?"

"Must be to get the little critters out of their hidey holes. You don't suppose they're still alive, do you?"

"I hope not. No. The bowl is warm to the touch. They've been cooked."

"What a relief. Lloyd, you try one first."

"Stacy, let me propose a toast." He held up his glass of iced tea. "Here's to good friendship. Let nothing come between us except the joy we feel in each other's company."

"I'll drink to that."

Lloyd picked up a dainty fork and poked it into one of the shells, retrieving a small morsel of something he'd once used as fish bait. After making sure the iced tea was handy and, after looking at Stacy, he closed his eyes and inserted it in his mouth. He did not chew into it at first, but ran his tongue over it to see if he could decipher how the beast was configured. Stacy waited to hear his opinion. He knew he would either have to swallow it whole or chew it into smaller bites. He chewed.

"Not bad. Good, actually." He reached for the bread. Breaking off a small piece he dipped it into the melted butter, garlic, and spices. "But anything cooked in this would taste good."

Stacy dipped her fork into a shell and put it into her mouth without looking. She was pleasantly surprised and within minutes they had finished the entire dish.

"Mr. Stanky walked beside me. We'd just left Kress's Five and Dime when a man stepped out of an alleyway telling us to stop. We turned around and saw he had a gun pointed at Edwin. He walked us into the alley and had me use a bolt cutter to break the chain going to Mr. Stanky's wrist. I handed it back while he asked for Edwin's handcuffs and key. He told us to put our hands over our heads and through a fire escape ladder hanging down the side of a building. He told me to put the handcuffs around our wrists and clamp them shut. With the bank's satchel, he walked to the end of the alley, which was about thirty feet. Edwin yelled that he knew him and he'd find him if it took the rest of his life. The man pointed his gun at Edwin and pulled the trigger. Edwin was hit in the chest. His knees buckled but he couldn't fall to the ground. I started crying. I'm not proud of that fact and haven't told anyone other than you."

"It's quite understandable. Had you seen the man before?"

"No. I held Edwin in my arms until help came. When I was freed, I started shaking. They let me sit in a squad car while I came to grips with what had happened. I gave my statement to Chief Trent, and an ambulance carried Edwin's inert body to the hospital."

"Lloyd, you've had a traumatic experience. When you've put everything into proper prospective, whatever other problems you might have will seem insignificant."

"I know. Before today, I thought I had so much going on I would lose myself in a haze if I didn't stay focused on my problems."

"What kind of problems do you think you have?"

"I now think they are too trivial to be of any consequence. Certainly not anywhere near the ones you're harboring."

A camera flashed. "Mr. Garrison, may I have a moment of your time? I'm with the newspaper and trying to make a nine o'clock deadline. Would you tell me what happened?" He paused then said, "Sir, you are news."

"Can't this wait? I'm having dinner with Miss Martin."

"And that would be Miss Stacy Jo Martin, head teller at the First Bank and Trust of Dancing Deer." The man wrote as he talked. To Lloyd he said, "Five minutes of your time and I'll make you a town hero."

"Go ahead, Lloyd. Opportunities like this don't come around every day."

The reporter pulled up a chair and motioned for the waiter to come over. He ordered a draft beer and said the newspaper would pay for the meal. Lloyd told his story a third time—leaving out the part about crying. The reporter wrote it down and turned to Stacy Jo. "Miss, do you have anything to add?"

"Only that Edwin Stanky is a very nice man. He's one of the reasons the citizens of Dancing Deer don't have any more crime than they do. Right now he's fighting for his life in Intensive Care and everyone needs to include him in their prayers."

"Very nice, Miss Martin. Thank you both." The reporter put his notebook into his pocket and hurried to the door.

Lloyd cut a big bite of his chicken-fried steak and said, "All right, it's your turn. Tell me about the Gilded Lily."

"The Gilded Lily? Lloyd, that's a house of prostitution."

"Yes, I know."

"You don't want to go there. A man as nice looking as you and with your prospects shouldn't stigmatize his reputation. Go to college, gather credentials, and meet a nice girl who'll appreciate you for who you are, for what you've done, and for the opportunities lying at your feet. The men who go there are . . . are not the sort you ought to hang around with."

131

"All right, but tell me what's it like there."

"As far as I can tell, there are six regular girls and another six who work part-time in the hopes of becoming one of the regulars. They live in town and get delivered by automobile each afternoon. A trick goes for ten dollars and each man has to be checked by a retired nurse the first time he visits. He purchases wooden tokens from the madam, and then goes into the front room to ogle the girls. When he finds one he likes, he strikes up a deal and then is led upstairs to a vacant bedroom. Usually, he'll leave a tip if he liked what he bought. That's all I know and more than you should."

"Okay. What about Boyd?"

"This is your last question. Boyd was my boyfriend for a year and a half. I found out he went to the Gilded Lily and I burned his clothes. I haven't seen him since."

"That was a little drastic, don't you think?"

"Certainly not. I'll not have a man who frequents a whorehouse."

"What if a man wants to date one of the women who work there?"

"I can't think of a more ridiculous situation. Now I've got to go. I promised Gladys I'd tell her how her husband got shot. Thanks for the information, Lloyd."

"Don't mention it. If you see Boyd tell him I tried but was unsuccessful."

CHAPTER 33 – THE DRAW OF THE CIRCUS
Friday early evening, December 21, 1945

"Why do we have classes? The kids in town are out until after the first of the new year," asked Judd. He was nine and had been at St. Bartholomew's Orphanage since he was found abandoned at Big John Lynch's gas station. Just a few days old, he was wrapped in a soft blanket and placed in a wicker basket, like fruit given as a Christmas present.

"Those other kids aren't learning anything. They attend class, but the teachers are just babysitting. I've heard they don't start algebra until the seventh grade," said Terrell.

"Man, Father O'Reilly started us in the third. What about science?"

"Don't know but it's probably about the same." Tyrone got up from his bench and walked to the window looking out over the church courtyard. "I don't know about you guys, but I'm ready to leave and see if I can make it on my own. With the girls visiting, we're the only ones available for the nuns to be nasty to."

"And where would you go?"

"I'd find that circus that came to town last September and get a job feeding their animals."

Spencer shut the book he was reading, stretched his arms high over his head, yawned, and said, "I wonder what the town would say if we all left?"

"That would solve the church's problem, if nothing else."

"Terrell, why do you reckon the town has shunned us in favor of the girls?"

"Because town-folk need different kinds of chores done. On a farm, there're lots of manual labor for a boy to do, but in town the work's mostly inside and centers in the kitchen. We can probably be thankful no one wanted us. The girls are now washing dishes, cleaning stoves, dusting furniture, washing clothes, and ironing. We don't want to do none of that."

"Penny told me she was planning on working hard so her family would want her to stay."

"Yeah, well, Laurie might have something to say about that. The family took both girls and said they might keep one. I guess the girls will start out being as nice as they can, doing everything they're asked and, as the time goes on, they'll start bad-mouthing each other to the family. I wouldn't be surprised if the family doesn't bring them both back."

"Spence, could you help me with this problem? I'm having the dickens of a time finding both factors."

"Sure."

"Lacy, I understand you received a Christmas card from someone in Ohio. Was it from a long-lost relative?"

"No. I got a pen pal. I found his name in the *Grit* newspaper. He said his dad took him to town and gave him ten dollars. They spent the entire day shopping for presents for everyone in his family. His dad went with him but didn't tell him how to spend the money. He said he bought everyone in his family a nice present saving the one for his dad till last. And when he was down to it, he didn't have any money left. So they went home and his father thinks he forgot. Now my friend is looking under seat cushions and seeing if any of his friends want to buy any of his toys." Lacy lowered his head so the other boys couldn't see the water filling his eyes. "Terrell, I miss my dad."

"I know you do, Lacy. We're your family now." Terrell put his arm around Lacy's shoulder.

"Okay, if one goes, we all go."

Father O'Reilly came into their room and said, "What have you boys decided to do as far as Christmas presents for the girls?"

"We've been whittling doll furniture from scraps of wood we found at Ridley Field. Lawrence, bring over one of the sacks so we can show Father what we've got."

From under his bed Lawrence grabbed a pillowcase and brought it over to the table, where he proudly emptied its contents. There were square blocks whittled down and painted to resemble stoves, wringer washing machines, refrigerators, radios, automobiles, beds, chairs, sofas, tables, and lamps. "We got two more sacks. We planned on divvying them into separate piles and putting in front of each pile a small street sign with a girl's name. What do you think Father? It was Terrell's idea."

"Terrell, someday you'll work for a large company and be their head cheese over sales."

"What does a head cheese over sales do?"

"He figures a way to present the company's products in such a way that the people purchasing feel they must have it—no matter what it is. They say some of the best can sell ice to Eskimos.

"Have any of you given the girls any ideas of what you'd like to receive?"

"No."

"I guess you're stuck with whatever they can come up with. Should be something nice though. I think last year they made kites from scraps of fabric. Tyrone, you got yours high in the air."

"Yeah, but most were too heavy."

"It's neither the expense of the gift nor how well it's crafted that matters. It's the expression of love the gift signifies."

Lacy raised his hand, "Have you heard if Mr. Stanky is going to be okay?"

"He was still in Intensive Care when I left the hospital. Doctor Rayne got the bullet out but told me Mr. Stanky needed our prayers. He said it was up to God now. And that, gentlemen, is from a man who struggles with his belief in God."

"So I want everyone to mention Mr. Stanky in his bedtime prayers. Tomorrow we're going to wrap presents at a few of the retailers. Goodnight, boys."

CHAPTER 34 – ADIOS
Friday night, December 21, 1945

"Just take what you want to haul. Clothes first. Be sure and put in all your socks and underwear."

The boys had decided to leave. Dancing Deer didn't want them. It was time to go. They were using their pillowcases as suitcases and planned on tying the openings shut and attaching short lengths of rope. They'd then hang the pillowcases over their shoulders and hold on to the ropes.

After Father O'Reilly left they portioned out the doll house furniture and wrote the girl's names beside each pile. They hadn't had time to make the planned street signs.

The boys left at the witching hour of midnight. Everyone in town was in bed except for the people putting together Saturday's edition of Jesse's newspaper. The boys decided to throw off any attempts to locate them by leaving a red herring on the south edge of town. In a pillowcase, they put an assortment of clothes they had planned on leaving and tied the ends together. It would be left under a street sign. Terrell spent an hour hauling it to the south side of town before coming back to the church and, with the other boys, heading west.

Lacy had his crutches, but Terrell decided to bring the Red Flyer and pull his crippled friend. From the kitchen, they loaded another pillowcase and placed it in the wagon with Lacy. This entourage trudged to the outskirts of a town soon to be ravaged by guilt.

Gladys was still in the waiting room when the shift changed. An hour later Stacy Jo came in and relayed the story Lloyd had given her. "Gladys, will you be staying the night?"

"Yes. I won't leave his side until I know he'll pull through. We've been through some difficult times and he was always there for me."

"Is there anything I can get you?"

"No. Thanks anyway, Stacy. But I want you to know that a person cannot do anything so bad that he shouldn't be forgiven if he truly repents."

A few minutes later the admitting clerk came down the hall carrying a clipboard. "Gladys, we've taken Edwin to a private room. He's stabilized somewhat. His heart is now beating in a rhythmic pattern. He hasn't gained consciousness, but the doctor thinks he's cleared the first hurtle. Will you be staying the night?"

Gladys felt like God had answered her prayers. With tears rolling down her cheeks, she nodded.

"There's a comfortable chair in the room and I'll bring you a blanket. Have you had anything to eat?"

"I'm not hungry. I'll be fine. May I see him now?"

"Sure, honey. Just follow me."

Fifteen minutes later, Gladys stood beside her sleeping husband. "Edwin, I know you don't think I love you. I haven't been the good wife you told everyone I was, but I will be."

Gladys smoothed the wrinkles on his blanket and took his hand in hers. She could swear she felt him trying to squeeze her hand, but maybe that was only her wishing it to be true. She looked at his smooth face and ran her fingers through his hair. Several strands had been hanging low on his brow. She put her hand to his forehead. No fever.

"Why did you tell that man you'd come after him? He probably wouldn't have shot you if he didn't think he'd be running from you for the rest of his life." Gladys carefully placed his hand alongside his thigh and sat in a big chair. In minutes, she was sound asleep.

"Let's put the picture of the alley with the handcuffs hanging from the bottom bar of the fire escape right here. Over here will be the picture of Edwin in his police uniform accepting that award the city gave him last year. And here in the middle will be Gladys asking everyone to pray that he pulls through."

"How about the picture of Lloyd and his girlfriend eating?"

"I don't know. It looks like they're having a good time when all the other pictures ask the reader to grieve with Gladys. We'll stick it on the next page along with the picture of the man's accomplice in the Skunk Hollow bank robbery.

"The only interview I'm not happy with is the one at the hospital with this Lenny character."

"I'm sorry about that, Jesse. The police wouldn't let me ask the questions, just stay in the room while they talked with him. They think he's a flight risk."

"Or that his friend will show up and try to cut him free. Now that he has plenty of money, they're probably thinking he'll want to spring his friend before leaving the area for good.

"On the last page, put the story about the families hauling the girls home for the holidays. Beside it, put the one about the neglected boys. We would have gone front page with that story had it not been for the robbery."

CHAPTER 35 – COLD, NEGLECTED, AND WORRIED

Very early Saturday morning, December 22, 1945

The snow stopped. Large piles had collected against anything with a northern face. The arctic winds shoved it there in drifts.

The boys had changed from the highway to a county farm to market road because hiding every time a headlight appeared in the distance had gotten old. So when a junction appeared, they decided they'd make better time heading a little north over a less traveled road. They'd go west again tomorrow. It was four a.m. when they started looking for shelter. The outline of Dancing Deer's water tower was still close enough to dominate the dark horizon.

Climbing a fence the boys traversed a white desert interspersed with frozen vegetation, broken limbs, and the occasional discarded farm implement. Soon they spied a building standing by itself in a clump of leafless trees. The building had broken window panes, a missing door, and numerous missing floor boards. Broken pieces of furniture, glass fragments, and empty feed sacks littered the building's interior. And several holes in the roof allowed in rays of light from a waning moon.

"Brrr. Is it warmer in California?" Lawrence let his pillowcase drop to the floor.

Terrell said, "Spencer, you stay here with Tyrone and Judd. See if you can find something to cover those two windows. We'll help you with the door when we get back." Terrell set Lacy down on the side of a wooden box. He and Lawrence left Spencer, Lacy, and the two younger boys, to retrieve the food from the wagon.

"Terrell, I don't mean to complain, but I'm thinking we should have waited till summer."

"Nonsense. As Father O'Reilly would say, 'It's mind over matter.' Besides, we don't actually have to go anywhere. We just have to draw attention to our situation. If we can stay lost through Christmas, we'll make an important statement."

"We could freeze before Christmas—or starve."

As they walked back to the decrepit farm building, they covered any signs they had made on the ground. Terrell pushed the wagon into a hole beside a hollowed out stump. Then he covered it with debris to make it look like it had always been there.

When they arrived back at the building, Spencer and the two younger boys had stuffed wadded-up feed sacks in the broken window panes. Spencer leaned a slab of wood against the back wall. "Look what I found."

"You brought a flashlight?"

"Yep. You said to only bring what we needed. I got candles as well."

"You bring any clothes?"

"Yeah, but my bag's so heavy I had to use two lengths of rope in a criss-cross over my back."

Lawrence said, "Whatcha got there? Can we prop it up to keep the wind from coming through the door opening."

"That's what I'm saying. This is the old door. It's still got the bottom hinge on it."

"Stick it in the opening and let's fix something to eat."

In thirty minutes everyone but Terrell was sacked out. They were wearing their clothing and wrapped in the blankets they had swiped from their beds. Terrell lay on his back looking up at the calm, clear sky through a hole in the roof. He decided this was where they'd spend Christmas. He had three dollars in change he'd been given when helping women with their packages. Tomorrow he'd walk to Cakebread and buy groceries. That and melted snow should be enough to see them through Christmas. Then they'd walk into town and say California was closed. They were now headed to New York City and needed more stuff.

At six, Ivan was shutting down the presses. He had printed five thousand copies of the *Marsden County Meteor*. It was time for a break. Jesse himself had managed the folding apparatus. The papers, stacked and bound, were waiting for the truck to take them to the points where the newspaper boys picked up their allotments and threw to the doorsteps of Dancing Deer citizens. After the newspaper boys, the truck headed to the neighboring towns where deliveries were made to restaurants and a few of the newfangled racks Jesse had a welder build. The truck returned to Dancing Deer for its final deliveries to stores and restaurants in its home town.

"Man, I'm glad that's over with." Ivan took out his handkerchief and wiped his forehead. "Jesse, let me help you with that."

"Nonsense, Ivan, I'm almost finished. You go sit down for a bit. I could take a glass of water before you get settled though."

"You got it, boss."

Jesse was proud of their achievement. The robbery had happened the day before and his paper—in only one day—conducted twenty-five interviews, took fifty pictures, and wrote three large articles and seven short ones. If the police force was as effective as his newspaper, they would have had the robber already locked up. When the last bundle was tied together, there was a collective whoop with several people slapping hands.

"I'm going home and sleeping till Monday."

"I was supposed to take my wife to Little Rock to do some last-minute shopping but she can kiss that goodbye."

"Jesse, what about you? You and your missus got anything special planned?"

"No. She's too close to term for us to go anywhere. My father-in-law arrived yesterday. He'll be with us until she delivers, then he's headed home to France."

"Where's he been since Bill Potter's trial?"

"The western half and the southern third of the United States. He bought the biggest car I've ever seen and has been on a joy ride for half a year."

"Man, what a life."

Jesse continued with, "Yeah, he doesn't say much about what he's done, but a smart person can piece it together. I think he was a spy in both world wars, he's been a race-car driver, and loved more women than Don Juan. I'd say that he's led an impressive life." Jesse abruptly stood up. "Okay, somebody lock her up. I'm outta here."

Jesse walked to his car. He was dog-dead tired. He had not pulled out of his parking space when a police car whizzed past, followed by another.

I wonder what's happened? Maybe I should join the chase. Maybe they've caught the robber. He opened his car door and stood on the one foot he exited with. "Anyone got a camera?"

Several people were right behind Jesse entering their vehicles. Mitzi had her key in the lock to the newspaper's front door. A man ran over and handed Jesse his camera and a new roll of film. Jesse headed west on Main Street. He didn't have far to go. Both police cars sat outside St. Bartholomew's Holy Catholic Church.

Jesse parked his car and walked to the front door. It was locked. He then walked toward the rectory but stopped when he saw light coming from the windows of the orphanage. He tried the door and went inside.

"So what did you do then?" asked one of the police officers.

"I looked under the beds, and then went to tell Father O'Reilly."

"Father, did the boys say anything that would lead you to believe they would be running away? Have you received any disturbing news in the mail? Any letters from relatives?"

"No. But, I knew they were not happy. We were going to wrap presents for the shoppers today." Father O'Reilly walked toward the door and held out his hand to Jesse. "Come in Jesse. You'll need to know the particulars for your paper."

Officer McRae held out his hand. "Good morning, Jesse. You look like I feel. You work late getting out the paper?"

"Yeah."

Officer McRae turned back to Father O'Reilly. "Did the boys take anything with them?"

"Most of their clothes are missing, the blankets from their beds, and a bit of food from the kitchen."

The policeman handed a note to Jesse as he wrote down the items missing. It read:

We're sorry for any trouble we've caused. We've left so the church won't have to spend anymore money on us. Now, that the girls are with the Dancing Deer families, we decided it was time to make our mark on the world.

Father O'Reilly, you are the only one we'll miss. You were kind and never talked down to us. But we do have one comment to make on your teaching skills. More history, a second language (preferably Spanish), and more modern science, with less math.

Thanks for everything. See you in the movies.
Terrell, Spence, Lawrence, Lacy, Tyrone, Judd

Jesse said, "May I copy the note?"

"Sure. We don't expect any foul play. You want a list of the items they took with them?"

"Yes. Anything you have would be appreciated. Does anyone have an idea of their time of departure?"

"No. Everyone here turns in early. They could have left as soon as it got dark. Where do you think they're heading?"

"California," said Jesse, "to become movie stars."

Chief Trent shook his head. "And they left three days before Christmas. We'll find them, Father. You don't have to worry none about that. A troop of six little boys. They'll stand out like a swollen thumb. We'll probably have them back before lunch."

CHAPTER 36 – THE TOWN REELS
Saturday morning, December 22, 1945

Connie Wiggins was the first one up. She thought about waking the girls but decided against it. She'd let them sleep in. After all, it was Saturday. She started a pot of coffee and opened the refrigerator to see what she could make for breakfast. When she closed the refrigerator door, two sleepy-eyed little girls stood in the doorway.

"Goodness gracious, what are you two young ladies doing up so early?"

"We always get up at six."

"Would you rather sleep till seven?" Both little girls nodded their heads.

"Let me give you a glass of milk. Then I'll take you upstairs and tuck you in. We usually sleep in on Saturday mornings."

There was a knock on the front door. Connie hesitantly walked over, wondering who would call at this time of the morning. It was still dark outside. After looking out the window and seeing a police car, Connie went straight to the door. "Good morning, Officer. Can I help you?"

"Mrs. Wiggins, I'm sorry to bother you so early. I saw your light and wondered if I might ask a couple of questions. Actually, I guess I need to direct the questions to Penny. Is she up yet?"

"Yes. But what is this about?"

"The boys have run away from the orphanage. One is Penny's brother. I just want to know if he told her anything. We'd like to bring them back as soon as possible. This is no weather to be walking somewhere."

"Come in, Officer. We're in the kitchen. Did they leave last night or early this morning?"

"We don't know, ma'am. Which one is Penny?"

A little girl meekly raised her hand.

"Penny, did Terrell say anything about running away?"

"No. He wouldn't leave me without letting me know. We've always been together. He's the one who carried me to the orphanage in the first place."

"Can you tell me if this is his handwriting?"

"It looks like his. But I'm not sure."

"Penny, if he gets in touch with you, would you please let us know? It's not safe for him to be on the streets. People don't know how to drive on ice. If we don't find him soon, we're afraid someone will get hurt. This Lacy kid can't even walk."

"Officer, if Penny's brother comes around or calls we'll phone you immediately." Mrs. Wiggins looked at Penny, who nodded her head.

Adelle didn't want to mess up her kitchen so when Claude came to pick her up for their trip to Little Rock, she suggested they go to the Ritz Bistro for breakfast.

"I'm telling you, those boys can take care of themselves. There ain't no need to worry for their safety."

"I don't know. I wouldn't want my boy walking anywhere this time of year. Man, it's snowing out there. And it's Christmas. What're they gonna do about Christmas?"

A fourth man walked from the breakfast buffet table with a plate of biscuits smothered in cream gravy, scrambled eggs, and sausage links. He set his plate down, turned up his coffee cup, and was about to go back for a large orange juice. "I'll tell you what I think. I think they're lonely. No one to spend the holidays with except each other. The paper says families have come to the orphanage and taken home the girls, leaving the boys to fend for themselves. I think they thought it was another blow delivered by fate, and they linked hands and headed for somewhere they would be loved and appreciated. It's not like we've been overly hospitable. I, for one, feel damn sorry for not helping when I had the chance."

"And what could you have done?"

"Let me get my orange juice and I'll tell you."

Claude pulled out a chair for Adelle. To the table of the three remaining gentlemen, he said, "What's this about the orphan boys?"

"Good morning, Claude. They ran away. Left last night. Left behind a note saying they didn't want to be a burden to the church or to the town anymore."

"And they left in this weather?"

"Yep, with a blanket and what few clothes each one had. Makes me shiver to even think about it."

"What are the police doing?"

"What can they do? They got all the squad cars covering the roads leaving town, so now, they're looking for the boys as well as the robber. The sheriff's department has the rest of the county to look through."

One of the three men said, "I think they should slide the capture of the bank robber to a back burner. I want them to find those boys. Every time I had any dealings with them they were polite, asking how my day was, carrying my wife's packages. I'm thinking about loading up some of this food and going looking for them myself."

The man going after the orange juice returned. "I thought about hiring one to help me do electrical work. Father O'Reilly asked me if I'd talk to them about being an electrician, but I said I didn't have time. I was being plain damn selfish. I could've talked to them one night a week for a month or so, wired up some contraption as an illustration, and then hired the oldest as a helper. I feel plumb bad."

The quiet one at the table said, "You're gonna go looking for them?"

"You know it."

"I want to go with you. My wife brought home this little girl named Millie. Her brother's one of the boys. We should have gotten him as well."

"Good. I'll ask the waiter if he'll put us some food together cause we're not coming back without 'em."

"Adelle, I can't go with you to Little Rock. I have to stay here and help find those boys."

"Claude, honey. I'm glad you feel that way. I wouldn't want you to be any other way. Maybe there's something I can do to help."

Three men walked in dusting off snow from their coats and hats. They walked to a table and plopped down. "Coffee, please."

One of the four seated men stood and walked to their table. "You fellas looking for the man who shot Edwin or the boys?"

"Both. Someone shoots a Dancing Deer citizen and I got to do something. Someone come and live in our little town and leave because we didn't open our arms to give a warm welcome and I got to make amends. I'm not by myself. A dozen cars are combing the roads looking for those boys. Dancing Deer wants a second chance."

CHAPTER 37 – THE MEN MAKE PLANS
Saturday morning, December 22, 1945

By eleven o'clock Boyd, Faisal, Harold, and Mayor Bob had been up for thirty minutes. They sat around Boyd's dining-room table in their underwear playing poker. They were on a short break while Boyd was looking through his house for something they could use for chips. Harold was now holding all the matches in a sizable pile.

"Listen, Boyd, you don't know what it's like. The women hate us. We say we want fried potatoes and we get rice casserole. We want to have everyone over for poker and ask the women to prepare some fixings. They raise so much hell we have to cancel the event altogether. You know, I think that's what they want. Raise a passel of objections, and then browbeat us into submission."

Harold relaxed into a more comfortable chair after retrieving the newspaper from the front porch. "Hey, guess what's in the paper?"

"What?"

"Someone shot Edwin."

"What?"

"It says right here Friday—yesterday—Edwin Stanky and Lloyd Garrison were robbed as they collected deposits from the town's merchants. The man escaped with a briefcase full of money in a black Ford. Edwin's in the hospital. They're not allowing visitors." Harold looked up. "Must be damn serious."

"Was Lloyd shot too?"

"No. Just Edwin. The thief handcuffed them together in an alley. Their hands went through a fire escape ladder attached to one of the buildings. He shot Edwin as he left and Lloyd had to hold him up until help came."

"Damn. Any witnesses?"

"Yeah, but no one recognized him."

"Look at this picture of Gladys. Do you think your old lady would stay at your side if someone put a hole in your chest? Imogene would be at Jellico's office to make sure my will was up to date," said Harold.

"I'll tell you what Clarice would do. It'd make her so mad; she'd take my gun and go looking for him. She wouldn't be doing it for me but because the culprit did something to something belonging to her."

"Yeah and Ophelia would try to join up with the man. According to her way of thinking, that would be the easiest way to bring him to justice: hang out with him, rob a few banks, and shoot a few people until she had enough evidence to turn him in."

Harold flipped the page. After a few minutes, he said. "Damn, they slid through the cracks."

"What're you talking about now, Harold?"

"The boys in the orphanage. Jesse's written an article saying Dancing Deer families have taken all of the girls into their homes for the holidays, leaving six of the seven boys."

"So what did you mean by sliding through the cracks?"

"What the hell do you think I mean? The church has seventeen children needing a home. It's Christmas time for God's sakes. Families grabbed up the girls and left the boys. What do you think those boys are thinking? I'll tell you what they're thinking. No one loves them. No one wants them. No one cares one hoot whether they are okay, if they would like company for the holidays, if they need anything—or anybody. Two of the boys had their sisters picked up, but the families didn't want anything to do with them. I think the people of Dancing Deer have let them slip through the cracks. We weren't even aware we were mistreating them."

There was a knock on the door. Boyd walked over and opened to Johnston Baker.

"You guys hear about Edwin?"

"Just what's in the paper."

"How about the boys from the orphanage?"

"Yeah, we were just talking about them as well."

"Then what're you doing here—in your underwear? Haven't you seen the cars whizzing past. The entire town's looking."

"Looking for the man who shot Edwin?"

"No. The entire town's looking for the boys. You guys don't know do you?"

"We don't know nothing Johnston. We got drunk Thursday night and had to have a taxi bring us to Boyd's. Friday we didn't start moving till noon and spent the entire day playing cards. Today we're just now getting around. What should we know?"

"The boys from the orphanage left. They gave the town ample opportunity and, when it didn't respond, they packed their things and headed to . . . to . . . some other town."

"And the cars are the town citizens trying to find them?"

"Yeah, word passed from one person to another. You fellas are probably the last to hear. The women have set up a command post at the library. We have to go there to be assigned a segment of town to look through. Others are given a road out of town to travel. Clarice has taken charge. Everyone's been asking about the four of you and the ladies are saying you're driving around on your own."

"How many boys are there?"

"Six. One of them can't walk. They left sometime last night in the snow."

Boyd said, "Without a ride they can't have gone far. It's cold, the wind's blowing, and it's snowing off and on. And, you say, one boy can't walk? How does he travel? Someone carry him?"

"I saw him being pushed around in a red wagon once. And I think he's got crutches," said Johnston.

"You say Clarice has taken charge?" asked Mayor Bob.

"Yeah, she called Betty early this morning. They don't know where you guys are."

"They must not be looking too hard. No one's called. No one's come by. We're not hid out. They could have found us with the smallest bit of effort."

"Anyway, the women are coordinating things."

"Clarice says she's gonna run for mayor as my opponent." Mayor Bob jumped up from his seat. "Man, I got to get dressed and get involved. If I'm going to run against Clarice, I got to start making a presence. It may turn out beating Clarice will be the biggest accomplishment of my political career." Mayor Bob headed to the bathroom.

Harold brought the paper to Boyd. "Looks like Jesse got a picture of Stacy Jo and Lloyd on a date."

"Let me see that."

"Good grief, Boyd. Stacy Jo burned your clothes and went to work at the Gilded Lily. You should be upset by those things. Here, she's just having an innocent meal." Faisal stepped toward the kitchen and began refilling his coffee cup. "Nothing wrong with that."

"When I talked to Lloyd Thursday morning I told him about Stacy going to work at the Gilded Lily. He thought for a moment, and then asked how much I thought she'd be charging. I had to control my rage before I busted his lip. Now, he's seeing her socially—not hiding the relationship like before. Probably seeing if he can get for free what he's started saving his money to purchase."

"Let's go give him another talk. This time we'll tell him what kind of grief he can bring on himself for messing around with another man's woman."

Mayor Bob stood in the doorway to the bathroom. "Faisal, she's going to work at the Gilded Lily. Soon, she'll be any man's woman who's got an extra ten dollars and likes his women young and frisky. She'll be selling it to every man in Skunk Hollow—and quite a few from Dancing Deer."

CHAPTER 38 – MERLE
Saturday morning, December 22, 1945

Merle finally had the tire off and in the trunk. All he needed now was to have his spare repaired. He flew out of town after robbing two men picking up deposits from the retailers and had a flat at the city limit sign. He continued driving until the highway passed over the Big Pincy River. Leaving the highway on a gravel road, he ended up at a public boat launch and parked his car under the bridge. When he found his spare was also flat, he wrapped in a blanket and pondered what he'd do. He'd been in difficult circumstances before. This time he had a briefcase full of money and a need to get a tire repaired without being seen by authorities.

After spending the next hour trying to break into the briefcase, he jimmied the lock with a tire tool. It was full of envelopes. Each envelope contained checks and cash. Eight thousand two hundred dollars in cash and twice that, or more, in checks. Dark came early. With that much cash, he didn't need the car, but he couldn't leave it and ride the rails. They might trace the car back to him, and then they'd have a name to go with a vague description. What he needed was someone to get the spare fixed—in a hurry.

With the tire from the car chewed up from driving while flat, the next morning—Saturday morning—Merle began solving his problems. First he used cord from his trunk to fashion an over-the-shoulder strap for the briefcase. There was no way he was leaving his loot in the car while he pushed the spare up the gravel access road to the highway and on to the next town. It wasn't long before the highway intersected with a county road, and he veered down its path thinking there would be less of a chance encounter with someone in authority.

At noon, he was overtaken by a tall, spindly kid walking and pulling an empty red wagon. "Hey, kid, how far to the next town?"

"Not far, but it's closer to the one behind you."

"Yeah, I know, but I can't go back there. I left a woman promising to bash in my brains when she saw me next. I got to go this way."

"Mister, you been walking far? I haven't seen a stranded car."

"A right smart piece. Don't suppose I could hire you to take this tire into the next town for repairing? I'll give you ten dollars."

"Ten dollars?"

"That's right. Here's five right now and there'll be five more when you return."

"I don't know. The next town might be ten miles or more."

"Okay. How about twenty? Ten now and . . . oh hell, here's the entire twenty. You don't get that tire fixed, I'll thrash you good."

"Gee, mister, that's a lot of money. I'll get it fixed for you. Where do you want me to bring the tire after it's repaired?"

"You know that road going down to a boat launch right out of town?"

"Under the Big Piney Bridge?"

"Yeah. Lay it down in the ditch beside that road."

"You got it, but it'll be after dark sometime."

Merle turned over the tire to the kid and started walking back to his car. After a couple of hours the bridge appeared in the distance. He stopped on the side of the road to rest. Merle considered the possibility of the police finding his car and waiting for him. He climbed through a barbed wire fence and walked a big looping circle. He'd sneak up from behind and see if there was anyone at the car.

It wasn't long before he was lost. All the trees looked alike. Then the snow intensified, reducing visibility to a few yards. Merle needed to find shelter fast. His hands were freezing; his nose and ears were numb to the touch. An hour later, he was no closer to finding his car or even the barbed wire fence he had crawled over. Merle stumbled and fell a short distance to the bottom of a washed-out gully.

Clutching the briefcase, he tried to get up. His ankle had turned in the fall and swelled up so fast both sides of his foot were now hanging over the sides of his shoe. "Damn. Damn. Damn."

CHAPTER 39 – THE WOMEN TALK PEACE
Saturday afternoon, December 22, 1945

"Does anyone know why Stacy Jo was at the Gilded Lily?" asked Suzanne.

Imogene said, "Harold says she's starting to work there on weekends."

"Why would a nice-looking girl like Stacy Jo work in a place like that? There's got to be a sane reason."

"Maybe she likes it." said Betty.

"Harold says her mother is sick. Stacy probably needs the extra money for her care. He said she can make as much as fifty dollars a night."

"How the hell does Harold know these things?"

"He told me Faisal heard Stacy Jo talking to another prostitute. The men were there to see where we were. They weren't interested in visiting the ladies; they just wanted to get fed. They left right after we picked up Ophelia. Faisal dropped Harold off fifteen minutes after Suzanne dropped me. I believe him. In fact, I think it's time I forgive him as well. Suzanne, you heard Betts say they've not been there since their run-in with the men from Skunk Hollow."

Ophelia stood up so everyone could hear. "Yeah, when I kicked Faisal out, he went to Clarice's to commiserate with Mayor Bob. He didn't head to the Gilded Lily. And, when he found Bob, they both went to Boyd's, eventually picking up Harold. Then, instead of going to Skunk Hollow, they went to Snockered. I agree with Imogene. I say we start giving them a little action." Ophelia sat down to let the other women digest her appraisal.

"I'm having a hard time forgiving Rube," said Suzanne.

Clarice decided it was time to take charge. "Okay, I agree. It's time to put this all behind us and get things back to normal. But if we give in, do we simply announce it? Blurt it out like they just won the Irish Sweepstakes? Do we initiate the intimacy?"

"I know what I'm gonna do. I've planned it for weeks," said Summer.

"What is it?"

"I'm not going to say. I think each woman should do it in her own way. Oops. We better come back to this topic later. A car just drove up." Summer went to the door and opened to two of Dancing Deer's men returning from a search.

One of them said, "Sector four is clean. We're going to get a cup of coffee and warm a bit, and then we'll need another."

Mona Millhouse went to a large poster sitting waist-high on an easel. She penned in the names of the two men, the word "Cleared," and the time in the box labeled Sector Four. She then wrote on a scrap of paper the next city sector not yet assigned and its boundary streets.

Suzanne poured two cups and handed them to the two men. "We've got hot dogs and a plate of pastries. Help yourselves."

In a few minutes the two men picked up their new sector and headed out the door.

Clarice waited for the door to close and said, "Bob also heard Stacy Jo talking about working there. He doesn't think she's started yet. I think we ought to pitch in. A few dollars a week from each family, maybe a half day doing the laundry, or taking her mother to the doctor, would be enough to keep Stacy Jo from having to work at the Gilded Lily. Has anybody heard about the round of venereal disease they got going?"

Clarice waited for this new revelation to sink in, and then continued, "Gladys called me Thursday night and said Edwin had heard the men in Skunk Hollow were vomiting blood. Some had developed sores—maybe she said boils—anyway, they had them all over their bodies. He told her there's no known cure. We can't have Stacy Jo working at a place like that."

"Why doesn't she marry Boyd? He's got a prosperous plumbing business. He could afford to take care of her, and her mother."

"Because she burned his clothes and has started seeing a young squirt at the bank."

Another two men opened the door and walked in saying, sector seven was clean. They headed to the table with hot dogs while Suzanne poured two large cups of coffee. In a few minutes, they had their new assignment and left.

Clarice said, "Ladies, what if we told the men they had to help us get Stacy Jo and Boyd back together and, if they did, we'd show our appreciation in a very amenable way?"

"Problem solved."

"That's ingenious, Clarice."

"I'm for it."

"Me too."

The door opened. This time their husbands came in. Betty went over to Johnston Baker and, reaching up on her tiptoes, kissed him on his cheek. "Honey, no one has found those boys. Do you think they could have located a shelter somewhere? A little while ago someone came in with a pillowcase tied at the top holding boy's clothing. They said they found it on the south side of town. We had those sectors checked a second time but didn't find anything."

Mayor Bob said, "We got to get organized. What areas of town have been looked in?"

Clarice walked over to the poster. It was a rough drawing of Dancing Deer. It looked like a Cartesian graph with the X axis going along Main Street and the Y axis the highway going north to Jasper and south to Skunk Hollow. The interior segments were numbered with a colored border around each section's perimeter. Inside each blocked section were names and other information, depending on whether the people assigned had returned yet.

Clarice said, "Robert, all but six areas of town have been scoured, with the men searching saying they were clear. We expect four of these six to report back soon. The remaining two were assigned late. They won't be reporting for a couple of hours. That will finish the entire town."

"What about the roads leaving town?"

"The major roads were traveled and then the searchers started driving over secondary roads down to goat trails."

The front door opened and several burly men walked in. "We're from Skunk Hollow. You people missing some kids?"

"We sure are. Did you find them?"

"No, we came to help you look for them. We got tractors that can go anywhere. You got any areas without roads needing to be searched?"

Clarice stepped forward and held out her hand. "We certainly do. Glad you men came to help."

CHAPTER 40 – DOCTOR RAYNE
Saturday afternoon, December 22, 1945

R. Charles Rayne came to Dancing Deer through a philanthropic organization's *Reach-Out to Small Towns Without Doctors* program. The organization paid for his education with the stipulation that it could dictate where the doctor would locate his practice. After his internship, he started his career as a general practitioner in the small town of Dancing Deer. Over the next two decades the town grew, and so did the doctor. He grew professionally. Through lots of night-time reading and his own endeavor, R. Charles Rayne, M.D. became a surgeon *par excellence.*

However skillful a man might be with the scalpel, there was another side to being a doctor. He hated this part of the job. Edwin was not responding, and he had to tell Gladys.

Doctor Rayne walked slowly down the hall to Edwin's room. He had treated Edwin numerous times. Usually for stomach problems when Gladys used him as a guinea pig for a new recipe or for broken bones or abrasions when Edwin tried to do something he was too old or too reckless to accomplish. This was the first time he had treated Edwin for anything serious.

"Hello, Gladys. Have they made you comfortable?"

"Yes. As much as possible."

"Then we need to talk about Edwin's condition."

"Doctor, he just lies there. Sometimes his nose twitches but that doesn't last very long, and then he's back to a deep slumber."

"Gladys, Edwin's in a coma. We don't know much about them, but sometimes people are in comas for years and other times for only hours. Usually, it's the result of a head injury. In Edwin's case it was from lack of blood carrying oxygen to the brain. The bullet nicked an artery leaving the heart, and he lost a lot of blood before we could get it repaired." Doctor Rayne sat in a chair next to Gladys. He reached over and covered her hand with his. "Gladys, Edwin is fighting for his life."

"Oh, no. No. No. No. Doctor you've got to do something. You can't let Eddy die. I'm lost without him. He's the reason I get up in the mornings."

"Gladys, we're going to start giving him oxygen. He's lapsed into a deep coma. His heart has started beating slower and his respiration has dwindled so much we need to help him breathe."

"Is there not anything I can do?"

"Yes. You can go home, get some sleep, eat a meal, and come back here to be with him. Some of us in the medical profession believe limited cognitive abilities are available to those resting in comas. Gladys, he might be able to sense when you're here. He might know more than he can tell us. No one has ever come out of a coma and led us to believe this is true, but it might be because the knowledge never makes it to the area of the brain where long-term memory resides."

Gladys hung her head. "I'll do whatever you say, Doctor."

"Gladys, I don't want to get your hopes up. I have never seen anyone come out of a coma as deep as the one Edwin's in. If he does revive, he might even be a different Edwin. While he's comatose, there's no way of telling if the lack of blood caused any permanent damage. We'll have to wait to find that out. Gladys, go home. Take care of yourself. For the next few days, weeks, and possibly months, you'll have to be strong. Edwin needs you."

CHAPTER 41 – SPENCER BUILDS A FIRE
Sunday morning, December 23, 1945

Spencer stretched and rubbed the sleep from his eyes. Soon he looked for something to hold water. He needed to brush his teeth. Under his breath he said, "Just have to make do."

He took his toothbrush from his makeshift suitcase and squirted on a glob of refrigerated toothpaste. After a thorough brushing Spencer spit into a hole in the center of the floor where several boards were missing. He thought to himself, what we need is a fire—right here in this opening.

Slipping through the door, Spencer pulled it back into the door casing. He surveyed the area. Probably used for cattle grazing. Should have a water trough somewhere. He started looking in likely areas. During the previous afternoon and early evening, a heavy snowstorm had wiped out any tracks they had missed. He triangulated where the building sat using distant markers and searched for something he could use to hold the fire.

An hour later he came upon a windmill. It should have once pumped water into an immovable concrete basin; instead he found a galvanized tub someone had used as a substitute. Spencer pried the circular tub out of six inches of frozen dirt with the help of a broken tree limb and started dragging it back to their hideout.

A hundred yards shy of the cabin; he saw an arm sticking up from a gully washout. Spencer put the tub down and ran to the arm. A man lay in the gully clutching a brown satchel. He was covered with a thin layer of snow. The hole he was in was the only thing saving him from freezing. If, indeed, he was not already frozen. Spencer picked up the man's hand and felt a pulse. The man coughed.

"Here, let me help you up."

"You an angel?"

"No. I'm lost—just like you."

"I think you're an angel. I prayed for you."

"Okay, I'm Spencer. Angel, Second Class on assignment. You're my first. Can I help you walk?"

"No. I got a twisted ankle. Didn't they tell you that with your assignment sheet?"

"I'll be right back. I have to get more angels."

In a few minutes Spencer returned with Lawrence and Tyrone. They found a hefty stick for the man to use as a crutch and helped him to his feet. Before long five little boys and one dangerous man huddled around a galvanized tub containing a sizable fire. They had placed the tub in a hole in the floor and stacked several broken boards in a pyramid. A heavy piece of wire screen kept the wadded up feed sacks, they used to get the fire started, stay in the bucket.

The man sat on his satchel while his body warmed and the cobwebs cleared from his head. Tyrone came over with a loaf of bread and a jar of jelly. "Mister, we ain't got much but you're welcome to share."

Merle grabbed the loaf of bread and broke off a large chunk. "You wouldn't have anything to drink, would you?"

"No. A couple of us have cups but nothing to put in them."

"What're you boys doing here?"

"We've run away to become movie stars."

"And where would you go to be movie stars?"

"Somewhere in California. We got a friend living there. His name is Russell."

"How far have you traveled?"

Lawrence looked down so the man wouldn't know he was lying. "A hunnerd miles." He looked up to see if he could see any change in the man's expression. "What are you doing here?"

Merle was a gifted liar. He didn't have to look down. "Chased out of town by a widow-woman. She claims I proposed and wants the sheriff to make me marry her. I had to leave fast. I think the sheriff's actually looking for me right now. You boys can't tell anyone I'm here."

"We won't say anything, mister."

"What else you boys got to eat?"

"Muffins, some Polish sausage, sauerkraut, a box of raisins, cereal, and two jars of canned peaches."

"Gimme the sausage."

"Okay, but it's the only meat we got."

After talking with Doctor Rayne, Gladys went home and fixed a bowl of soup but couldn't force herself to eat. Constance Wiggins came over around six-thirty and brought the two little girls.

"Gladys, the girls cooked chicken and dumplings for you. Do you think you could eat a little? When I told them about Edwin being in the hospital, we decided we needed to fix your supper. They said they've never cooked anything. Can you imagine? Guess it's not part of their curriculum. Anyway, I told them you were one of the best cooks in the county and if you said what they prepared was good then we had accomplished a milestone. I showed them how, but they did the work. Could you at least try a bite?"

"I'm sorry, Connie. I don't have much of an appetite. But if they went to that much trouble then I ought to take a few bites." Gladys poured a bowl of the broth and ladled some of the chicken and two round dumplings on top. "Actually, this is excellent. You young ladies can cook for me anytime you want."

Constance told the two girls to go into the living room and play with their new dolls while she and Mrs. Stanky discussed grownup matters. "Gladys, those two girls are so precious I'm in a stew about what to do. Penny has an older brother who's lost in the snow. He's fourteen. I picked out Penny and Laurie without considering him. Now, Jefferson and I feel like we're part of the reason the boys ran away."

"You shouldn't feel that way, Connie. You did more than a lot of families did."

"Yes, I know, but still it isn't enough. Jefferson read the article in Wednesday's paper about Penny's brother so many times he's got it memorized. It all happened in a thunder storm. Penny's brother was in the barn milking when lightning struck their house starting a fire? He ran in and carried Penny out just as the roof caved in. Their farm was so isolated that no one knew. He buried both of their parents himself and carried Penny to the church. Father O'Reilly had to talk him into staying. That was seven years ago."

"He must be a brave little boy."

"We think so. As soon as the boys are found we're going to bring him home as well. The problem is, Gladys, how am I gonna tell Laurie she has to go back? We're not financially able to adopt all three. In fact, two will be stretching the budget. I was thinking maybe you and Edwin could offer Laurie a home. She's a sweet little girl. You should have seen her eyes when I bought her a doll."

"I don't think so, Connie. I've got so many problems right now. And I'm not handling any of them very well. Doctor Rayne said he's never seen a person who was in a coma as deep as Edwin's, to come out. He told me not to get my hopes up and, if Edwin did wake up, his brain might be affected. If Edwin lives, he might be an invalid for the rest of his life—not even knowing who I am."

"I'm so sorry to hear that. You know, Gladys, Laurie might be good for you. She's never known a life outside the orphanage. She was handed over by her mother as a newborn. They mature fast when having to overcome difficulties like that. She might be more of a help to you than a hindrance. Think it over. If you would like to have her around for a few days, I've promised Father O'Reilly I'd have them back after the first."

Both women walked into the living room. Penny sat in Edwin's chair combing her doll's hair with a tiny brush. Laurie was in Gladys' chair looking through a magazine. Her doll sat in a corner facing the wall. Both women looked perplexed at Laurie, who said, "She's been bad and will have to sit there for another couple of minutes."

CHAPTER 42 – THE MEN ARE GIVEN THE TERMS

Sunday afternoon, December 23, 1945

"Johnston, what do you think?"

"I think it's wonderful. Let's plan a party and invite both. I think nature will take its course. All we'll have to do is give them a gentle nudge and then we can all leave the party early to our own little party at our own house."

"The chair recognizes Harold."

"Mayor Bob, I think we have to do something fast, before the women change their minds. I also think that we don't have time to plan a party, get some entertainment, decorate a house, and cook some little doodads. Let's have it at the Ritz. They've already got a Christmas Eve Party planned. I say we call them up, have them put a few tables together, and *voila*—it's a done deal."

"I second the motion."

The men never argued much. Being six men with matching instincts, walking similar roads, searching for the same things, and impressed with equivalent criteria, it's easy to see how they could so easily come to the same conclusion. What was different about the men was that they had married women with differing needs. The men didn't understand the women and, as much as they tried, each effort to mollify the women usually ended in dismal failure. This time the women had been explicit in what they required and each man was ready to move mountains for the prize he would be awarded for accomplishing the deed.

"Okay, that's settled. Johnston, you're Boyd's best bud. Do you think you ought to ask him or do you prefer to ask Stacy Jo? You know her better than any of us since you and Betty have entertained Stacy and Boyd more than anyone else."

"I'll get them both there if you guys will pay my cover charge and meal."

"Done."

Tyrone walked over to Spencer. "We need something that'll hold water. We only got two cups and waiting for the snow to melt generates about a third of a cupful in each at most. If we had another galvanized trough like the one we're using for the fire, we could finally have some drinking water."

"I agree. Let me draw a map of the area as I know it, and each one of us can scour a part." Spencer tore open one of the feed sacks and ripped it into four pieces. With a stick he'd retrieved from the fire, he used the charcoal end to draw on each: the building, the barbed wire fence, the road, the windmill, and a few other landmarks.

"Okay, we need a bucket or some sort of container that'll hold water. While it's not snowing, let's see if we can find something that'll work. Pick out a landmark and walk straight to it. Try and follow a straight line. Look around the landmark. Be observant. Check both sides of your path but don't veer too far away. When you've checked out the landmark and the path to it, follow your footprints back here. Don't stay gone too long. There're wild animals looking for their dinner out there."

Judd said, "Spencer, don't you think I ought to stay with Lacy."

"Sure, Judd. You and Lacy keep our new friend company. We'll be back in a half hour or so."

Merle casually picked up Judd's map and slid it into his back pocket.

Ten minutes after they left Merle said, "All you boys related? Seems like you get along real well. Brothers maybe?"

"Nope. Just good friends," said Lacy. "We look out for each other. It's the only way we can get anything accomplished. Individually we're weak but united we're invincible."

"Do any of you have a family?"

Judd said, "I do, but the others don't." Judd didn't say anything for a moment. Then he reached up and wiped the corner of his eye. "I don't know where they are or what their names are. I got a postcard one year at Christmas, but it just said 'Love you, Mother.' And I have a picture." From his pocket, he took a little wooden box. "Spencer carved it for me." He opened a hinged lid and pulled out a waxed paper envelope.

"Here, see how pretty my mom is. That's my father. Funny looking hat, don't you think?"

Merle said, "I think my parents are still alive. I haven't seen them in years." He handed Judd the picture. "You need to put this back. I wouldn't want it to get damaged." Merle threw two pieces of broken furniture onto the fire.

"So none of you boys have any family. No one to spend Christmas with. You've walked a hundred miles and have just a little food. Aren't you scared?"

"No. We have faith to sustain us. Didn't you say you prayed for an angel?"

"Yeah. Silly, wasn't it? I would have died out there if you boys had not helped me."

"It's not silly at all. God asks us to challenge him. You ask him in the right way and he'll provide no matter what. It might not be for what you asked, but it will be for what you need."

"Your name's Lacy, right?"

"Yes, sir."

"What happened to your family, Lacy?"

"We were driving on a mountain road called the Pig Trail. There were lots of curves, sometimes with a cliff on one side and a deep chasm on the other. Dad swerved to miss a large boulder tumbling down the cliff. That's all I know. Everyone died but me. These guys are my family now."

"Don't you miss your old family?"

"Sure I do. At Christmas more than any other time of year. I dream about them sometimes. My mother used to sing to me before I'd go to sleep."

"How long ago did it happen?"

"This is my second Christmas without them."

"And the accident is the reason you can't walk?"

"Yes, sir. My ankle was crushed when the car landed on its side."

"So, Lacy, if you can't walk how did you make it a hundred miles?"

"Terrell pulled me in a wagon. Sometimes he carried me. He's my best friend."

"What have you done for him?"

"He doesn't make me do anything to pay for his friendship. He does things for others because he wants to. It's what Jesus said to do. Did you ever hear the story of the Good Samaritan?"

"I think so. A long time ago."

Lacy said, "In *Leviticus* 19:18 the Lord said we should love our neighbor as our self. Then in *Luke*, Jesus told the story of a man traveling to Jericho who was robbed, beaten, and left for dead on the side of the road. Soon after, a priest came upon the injured man, crossed to the other side of the road, and passed by.

"Then a Levite happened on the man and did the same thing. But a Samaritan felt compassion when he saw the crumpled body and tended to the man's wounds. The Samaritan took the injured man to an inn where he could better care for him. The next day he gave the innkeeper two denarii for the man's care and said if the innkeeper had more expense he would provide additional funds on his return trip.

"Terrell is doing for me what any decent person—whether Christian, Samaritan, or other—would do for his neighbor and what we have done for you."

"Lacy, I'm impressed—and appreciative. Maybe I should have been a better neighbor."

Judd tapped Lacy on the shoulder. "Lacy, tell the story of the son who comes home to his family after being separated for a long time and eats the fatted calf."

"Okay, there was a man who had two sons. One day the youngest son tells his dad he wants his inheritance. His father agrees and divides his wealth giving the youngest son his portion. The son leaves his family and travels far away. He squanders his money on loose living until he has nothing left. The friends, who he had spent his inheritance on, would not repay his generosity. When the son became destitute and could not feed himself, he got a job tending swine. He soon realized his father's hired men were better off than he, and went home. He planned on asking his father for a job, but when the father saw him in the distance the father was filled with compassion. He had a servant go tell the other family members, and he told his oldest son to kill the fatted calf. The father ran to greet his son for he had been lost and now he had returned."

"Why do you think the father forgave his youngest son so easily?"

Lacy threw a chair leg into the fire. He said, "Because a father's love has no bounds."

"Edwin, I'm here darling." Gladys walked to the bedside of her comatose husband. She picked up his hand and held it in both of hers. A shadow moved in the corner of the room. Gladys gasped.

"I'm sorry to frighten you, ma'am. I've been watching him and he hasn't moved for the past two hours. I just came in to talk with someone."

"Who are you?"

"My name's Lenny. I got hurt a few days ago and am just now able to walk. I'll leave you now. I sure hope he wakes up soon. I just wanted someone to talk with. I didn't mean no harm."

Lenny slowly walked past Gladys, turned left, walked past the admitting desk, and out the front door. In an hour he had purchased a ticket for a bus headed north.

Gladys pulled up a chair to Edwin's bedside. "Edwin, there's some things we need to talk about."

"Mrs. Martin, is Stacy Jo there?"

"She is. Is this Gerald?"

"No, ma'am."

"Patrick?"

"No. Mrs. Martin, my name is Johnston Baker. May I speak with Stacy Jo?"

"Mr. Baker, you have two last names. Do you love my Stacy Jo?"

"Uh . . . no. I'm just a good friend."

"Well, that's a relief. I got 'em taking numbers here. Just a minute and I'll get her ladyship."

In a few minutes, Stacy Jo spoke into the telephone, "Hello, this is Stacy."

"Stacy Jo, this is Johnston. We've been trying to get a hold of you. I decided to call you at your mother's on a lark."

"Merry Christmas, Johnston. You and Betty doing all right?"

"Better than all right. We're having a party. Every one of our debts to Bill have been paid. And we've made up with the women, so we're all going to celebrate with a big party at the Ritz tomorrow night. Stacy Jo, you have to be there. It's mandatory."

"Mandatory, you say? Will Boyd be there?"

"I haven't said anything to him yet, but he will probably be there. Unless he's already got a date. Since this is the only party in town, I'm sure he'll be there. Can I count on you coming? You're welcome to talk with Clarice or Betty if you have any doubts.

"The women told us they wanted to be wined and dined. We've even agreed to dance. Harold didn't want to go that far, but Imogene gave him a look that would boil ice water and he quickly agreed. It should be hilarious to watch."

"Let me talk to Betty."

"Sure."

"Hello, Stacy. It's just like my John said. We're over our problems with the men and we're celebrating tomorrow night at the Ritz. Did he tell you Harold is going to dance with Imogene?"

"Yeah."

"You sure don't want to miss that. I'll save you a seat next to me, honey. What do you say?"

"Okay. Save two. You know—just in case."

"You got it, honey. Be there at seven and bring a small gift."

"Listen, Betty, what's the last word on the orphan boys?"

"Nothing new. This town was scraped clean. All the roads were checked and some guys from Skunk Hollow took their tractors and went up both sides of the Big Piney and the Illinois Bayou. Someone must've given them a ride. Everyone's still upset, but we don't know what else we can do. When we called the Ritz to see if they had any seats, they told us half the seats they had already sold had called and canceled. We're going to discuss what else we can do at the party."

Sunday night Terrell walked in the front door with two large sacks of groceries. He saw the man and the boys huddled around a fire. To Lawrence and Spencer he gave the two sacks and sat down to warm his hands.

"Your spare is fixed and in the roadside ditch."

"Thank you. I got lost walking back and your friends found me in a hole covered with snow. I think it must have been providence that brought me into contact with you guys."

Lawrence and Spencer were into the two sacks. "Terrell, you got a cooked breast of turkey in here. There's lots of stuff, here's a tub of cranberry salad, and hot dogs. This is going to be the best Christmas ever."

"We owe it all to this man." Terrell pointed to Merle. "He gave me enough money for fixing his spare tire to feed us for a couple of weeks."

"Thank you, sir, for your generosity," said Lawrence.

"I wasn't doing it out of the kindness of my heart. I thought he was driving a hard bargain. I now think I should have given him even more money. Who knows, he might have brought back a stove and a refrigerator."

"I think we can keep things sufficiently cold without a refrigerator."

"Let's eat hot dogs tonight, and tomorrow we delve into a feast done up right."

After a meal of hot dogs cooked on sticks hanging over the fire and cookies and melted snow from a basin that looked a lot like a rusted chamber pot, the man entertained the boys with stories of what he'd done as a young man just about their age.

"Boys, this will be a memorable Christmas for all of us. Years from now when we're gathered in small family units singing Christmas carols and drinking eggnog we will think back to the wonderful time we spent seated around an open fire in a combustible-friendly cabin with big holes in its roof."

Merle continued, "These last several Christmases I sometimes get melancholic thinking about my family. I left them several years ago and have lost touch through my own self-centered pride. My father was a Methodist minister. I imagine he's now retired. We owned a small house in Ind . . . well, it doesn't matter where home is because we were seldom there. The governing body of our denomination sent Dad where his talents could be of best use. But, we all knew that someday Dad would retire, and when he did we had a place to go.

"When I was very young, even younger than you, Judd, I remember sneaking into the living room on Christmas Eve to see what

Santa had brought during the night. We had wrapped presents, but Santa's were unwrapped. My brother was two years younger than me and sometimes he got something I wanted. I had no qualms snatching a piece of paper with my name written attached to a pair of socks or some similar gift and placing the piece of paper on one of his gifts.

"On Christmas Eve we went to bed early and Jeff could never stay awake. I lay there waiting for Mom and Dad to go to bed so I could sneak in for a gander at Santa's gifts.

"I think my dad figured out what I was doing and one year set a trap. I waited as long as I could and then slowly opened my bedroom door and crawled out on my hands and knees. It took several tedious minutes for me to make it down the hall and into the living room. We always kept the house dark for sound sleeping and I sure didn't want to go bump in the night.

"I finally made it behind my father's favorite chair. I waited there for a long time to assure myself that everything was okay and that I would not get caught. I then started crawling, ever so quietly, around the corner of that chair toward the tree and all that wonderful loot. That was the moment I was caught. A hand reached out and sat on top of my head. I froze—too scared to cry out, too discombobulated to do anything other than freeze in my tracks.

"Someone had been sitting in Dad's chair—being just as quiet as me. After a moment of terror, I jolted back into my bedroom and hid under the covers.

"The next morning I asked my dad if that had been him. He looked surprised and said no that it was probably Santa Claus. He asked if I could not actually see who it was and I replied 'No, it was too dark.' He said, 'Well, see there, it really was Santa.'"

Soon everyone was drifting off. When the man curled up, he set his head on the satchel and pretended to fall asleep. In a few minutes, Terrell walked over and placed his blanket over the man and lay down beside the fire.

Looking into the flickering orange and red tongues Terrell said in a low voice, "Thank you Lord for the many blessings you have given us. I especially want you to watch out for our new friend. I think he's lost his way and is searching for something only you can provide.

"I also want to thank you for helping Lacy. I know how much pain he must be in. He's run out of medicine and I think he's been crying more than usual. The rest of us are holding up well under your protection and saving grace. Amen."

CHAPTER 43 – CHRISTMAS EVE
Monday morning, December 24, 1945

"Mrs. Stanky, did he threaten you in any way?"

"No. He was very polite. He apologized for scaring me, said he'd been watching Edwin for two hours. He only wanted someone to talk to. When he left, he walked slowly and favored his left side."

"Did he take anything?"

"He might have. Edwin always kept a few dollars, but now his pockets are empty."

"Thank goodness you're not hurt. He's the one who robbed the bank in Skunk Hollow. We think the man who was driving his getaway car was the man who shot your husband. They've probably linked up by now and are long gone."

"I don't know, Officer. He seemed genuinely interested in Edwin's condition. Edwin never carried much money. If he came in here to rob Eddy, why didn't he make me hand over what I had in my purse?"

"There's no way to know without asking him. We do know for sure he was the one who robbed the bank. He seemed a little daft—more like a child than a dangerous adult. If we apprehend him maybe we can find out." The officer put away his notebook. "Mrs. Stanky, how's Edwin doing? I've heard he's still in a deep sleep."

"Yes. They call it a coma. Doctor Rayne says he doesn't think Edwin will come out of it. I'm sick with worry."

"Ma'am, if there's anything we can do, please ask."

After the policeman left, Gladys turned on the hot-water faucet in the nearby sink. She soaked a small face towel in the spewing water and wrung most of it out before draping the warm and moist cloth over Edwin's face. From her purse she removed a few of his toiletries. Filling a bowl with hot water, she dipped in his shaving brush and then raked it across a cake of shaving soap. Soon Edwin's face was lathered and surrounded by the steaming towel. Gladys opened his straight razor and bent the handle counter-clockwise two hundred and seventy degrees.

177

With her left hand, she pinched the blade between her thumb and first two fingers. Gladys had never shaved anyone before but found Edwin a captive audience. He didn't move. She scraped the shaving cream from his face, using her thumb and index finger on her right hand to hold the skin taut. She rinsed the razor in the bowl after each stroke. Halfway through she replaced the water. After she had finished, she re-soaked the towel in hot water and wrapped it completely around his face leaving only enough room to re-insert the breathing apparatus.

"Honey, I'll get faster at this with more practice."

Carl Creighton opened his doors for the rush of last-minute Christmas shoppers. He expected this to be his busiest day. Besides his daughter at the watch counter, he positioned his wife at the cash register and had saddled her with the onerous task of wrapping presents.

Everything was set. They would open in fifteen minutes. Meredith asked her dad if he had heard anything about Edwin Stanky's condition.

"No. Nothing new. He was supposed to be in today to pick up his wife's present." Carl took a cotton cloth and wiped fingerprints from the glass case holding the wedding and engagement rings. He stopped. "Meredith, there's a package with Mr. Stanky's name on it with the layaways. Would you please bring it here?"

When she returned, Mr. Creighton took the box and opened the lid. "Magnificent. These are simply magnificent." He took out the piece of paper saying Edwin still owed fifty-eight dollars and marked it paid over his initials. He placed the paper in the cash register and handed the box to Mrs. Creighton. "Love, would you wrap this for me. I need to take it to the hospital before we get busy."

When Carl opened the door, Big Bear Radisson was sitting on a bench a few feet from the store's front door.

"Come in. We're now open for business."

"Thank you, sir. I have put off this purchase until the last minute."

"Mr. Radisson, I have an errand to run but I think my daughter can help you find a suitable gift."

Meredith was standing at her father's elbow. "Merry Christmas, Bear . . . uh, Mr. Radisson."

"Merry Christmas to you. Miss, have we ever met before?"

"We've never been introduced, but I have seen you on occasion. I was at the ball game when you hit that ball into downtown Dancing Deer to win the game. Would you like to see it? I have it sitting on a pedestal in my bedroom,"

"You do?"

"Yes. I posted a reward for it and the next day two children brought it into the store. They argued over which one had found it so I paid them both the money I had offered on the poster."

"Couldn't you have split the money between the two."

"I could have but I was so happy to have the memento that the money was of no importance whatsoever.

"Would you sign it for me?"

"Ma'am, I'm no one of importance."

"Yes you are. You're Big Bear Radisson and that's important to me. Now what is it you'd like to see?"

"My girl-friend is considering moving to West Virginia. There is a man there she has become infatuated with and I want her to change her mind and stay in Dancing Deer . . . with me."

"You're not buying her an engagement ring are you?"

"Not yet. I was thinking more along the lines of a gold bracelet or diamond earrings."

"You know, uh . . . Mr. Radisson, you can't buy love. It has to be freely given. If you really want her to stay, you have to . . . no forget that. Let me get you a tray of gold bracelets."

"No. I want to know what you were going to tell me."

"First you tell me how you were planning on giving her the gift."

"She's packing right now. Last night she called to say she had made up her mind and that she was sorry, but she was headed to West Virginia. So I need that gift right now."

"I'm sorry Mr. Radisson, I won't be able to sell you anything today."

"What?"

Two blocks away, Jesse Bell walked into Ava's Dresses. "Hello, Mona. I didn't know you worked here."

"Just filling in for Gladys. May I help you find something for Genevieve?"

"Yes, and I need to know if your seamstress finished letting out those dresses I brought in last week?"

"I believe she has."

"Good. Then I'd like to pick out six or eight of your latest fashions in a size six. Can you help me with colors and accessories? I'll need some shoes, a couple of purses, and a hat or two."

"Jesse, we can do all that for you, but don't you think Genevieve will need a couple of dresses in a size ten and then a couple in a size eight? She won't lose the excess weight all at once."

"Sounds reasonable to me."

"Will you need them gift-wrapped, Jesse?"

"That would be great."

For the next hour, Jesse and Mona coordinated Genevieve's post pregnancy wardrobe. When they finished, Jesse paid and said he'd be back in the afternoon to pick up the packages. When he left the store, he was passed on the sidewalk by Mr. Creighton.

"Merry Christmas, Carl."

Over his shoulder, Carl Creighton said, "Merry Christmas to you, Jesse."

Jesse came to a Salvation Army kettle and tossed in the change he had in his pocket. The man ringing the bell looked like the vagrant who had been sweeping the sidewalks the day before.

"Thank you, Mr. Bell. Merry Christmas to you, sir."

Jesse reached for his billfold and tossed in two folded bills. This was going to be a good Christmas. Now if someone could find those boys, the police apprehend the bank robber, and Edwin wake up. Jesse wondered if he was asking for too much. He smiled. It could happen, the day was still young and Christmas wasn't until tomorrow.

When Jesse made it to St. Bartholomew's Holy Catholic Church, he saw two people exiting as four others waited to go inside. Father O'Reilly held the door open.

"Merry Christmas, Father. You got people in line waiting to light candles?"

"Yes, Jesse. For Edwin and the boys. There's still no word on either."

"We have to be strong, Father."

"Yes I know. They are in God's hands."

"Harold, put your right hand here and use this hand to hold my mine. Between your thumb and first three fingers, Harold, we're not shaking hands. Now look over my shoulder, we don't want to be bumping into people. Take two steps forward and one step back. That's it, now do it again. We need to be making a big box with two steps forward and one step back on each side. That's it. Now, again."

"Imogene, can't we sit for a while? We've been practicing the same thing for over an hour."

"We can't stop, Harold. Now we need to do those steps to music."

"He'll embarrass you, Imogene."

"Mother Lucille, I'll do no such thing."

At the First State Bank and Trust of Dancing Deer, Boyd walked past Stacy Jo's window and plopped down his deposit at Thelma's window.

"Good morning, Boyd. You look good enough to eat. Are you doing anything special this Christmas?"

"Hello, Thelma. No, nothing unusual. You know how it is with plumbers. We have to slosh around in the mud and keep the pipes unclogged so everyone else can have a good time."

"So if I were to call you around seven and say my pipes needed some of your superior handiwork, you would come take care of me?"

"Thelma, you live in an apartment. You'd have to call your landlord and he'd call me."

"I can probably get that accomplished."

"Actually, I have other plans for tonight."

"Okay. What about New Year's Eve? They could break just as easily then."

The man in line behind Boyd said, "Thelma, if you would take my money, I'd be on my way and you and Boyd could discuss this all the way till next Thanksgiving for all I care."

Boyd walked out shaking his head while Stacy Jo's entire body was shaking, or, rather, trembling. No customers had been moving in either line, with Stacy's back turned to her tray holding a man's deposit. When Boyd left, business got back to normal with both lines moving again.

Stacy had a break at ten. She walked to Lloyd's office and knocked. "Lloyd, you got plans for this evening?"

The boys woke early in the morning and found the man was missing. So were the partial loaf of bread and both jars of canned peaches. What he had left were the satchel and a note:

> Boys, I took a few items for my breakfast. I would appreciate it if you would see that the Dancing Deer Police are given the briefcase. I robbed the bank but have started a new chapter in my life and want to give the money back. I'd take back that bullet if I could.
>
> Tell the police Lenny can't read. He reverses his numbers and letters. He didn't know what he was doing at the bank in Skunk Hollow. He was only giving the teller a note I badgered him into putting into her cash tray. He's still a child but in an adult body. He didn't know what was going on, other than the teller was going to give him our money.
>
> I took some spending cash for gasoline. I'll replace it when I get a job. I'm going home to spend Christmas with my parents and brother while I still can.
>
> Merry Christmas, boys. Don't think too harshly of me, for I've been rescued by an angel. (Albeit an Angel Second-Class on his first assignment.)

"Terrell, what should we do?"

"We can't keep the money and we can't give it to someone else to take back for us. The only thing I can think is to deliver it ourselves. Maybe there will be a small reward and we can use that to finance a trip to Florida. It stays warm there all year long."

Carl Creighton asked the admitting clerk if visitors were allowed into Edwin's room. She told him that Edwin was still in a coma but that the doctor had started allowing people to go in for short periods of time. She gave him directions.

While standing in the doorway, Carl heard Gladys talking to her husband.

"Edwin, I didn't get to buy you anything for Christmas. I had this elaborate scheme where I'd get a job and buy you a new wedding ring. Then when I realized how expensive they were and I would only have the job at Ava's for a few days, I tried to think of something more practical. I thought about another pair of deerskin house shoes, getting your dress shoes resoled, or another puppy. But this happened so suddenly that I haven't gotten you anything.

"Several people brought food to the house. There's also an entire basket full of cards and the orphan girls wrote letters. Here, let me read you the one from Laurie."

Dear Mr. Stanky,

I want to thank you for standing up to that bad man. Too many people give in to the bullies of the world. When we let them run over us, it feeds them and makes them think all people will roll over and expose their vulnerable spots.

Please get well. You are in my prayers. Father O'Reilly says only God knows when a person's time is up. He says we have to live our lives like each day might be our last and we don't want to leave with a vow not fulfilled, a promise not performed, a hatred not forgiven, a bad word not taken back, or a love not expressed. Father O'Reilly said that was the way you lived your life and, for that, you are my hero.

May I come and see you when you are better? I'm with Mr. and Mrs. Wiggins till the first of the year. I've overheard them talk about adopting Terrell and Penny, so I'll be going back to the orphanage.

I have a new doll. I named her Edwina. Hope you don't mind.

Love,
Laurie

Carl waited while Gladys folded the letter and stuffed it inside her purse. Then she tidied up Edwin's covers. When he thought enough time had passed, Carl knocked and said, "Excuse me, Mrs. Stanky."

"Hello, Mr. Creighton. Come in. Is there any word about the boys yet?"

"No, I don't think so. Here, I have something for you," Carl held out his package, "Edwin made a purchase at my store and he wanted me to hold it for him till Christmas. He was supposed to pick it up today. He said it was your Christmas present. I had my wife wrap it. Do you have any children? I have a gift back at the store that's lost its tag. It's for a child."

"Thank you, Mr. Creighton. No, we don't have anyone, except each other. Not yet anyway."

"Oh, well, I'll keep looking. I seem to remember a name . . . Laurie, maybe?"

"I do know a Laurie. Mr. Creighton, could it be for one of the orphans?"

"Yes. He said it was for a little girl who didn't have much. A funny looking man: short, stocky, elderly, but with a spring in his step and a smile on his face."

"Mr. Creighton, that sounds like Santa."

"You're right. Now that I think about it he did look like Santa. If you have time to come by the store I'll have it by the register and you can give it to the little girl next time you see her. It's already paid for, Mrs. Stanky." Carl walked to Edwin's bed and patted him on the shoulder. "You know I consider Edwin, a personal friend. I am with the rest of the town in wishing him a speedy recovery. Is there anything I can do to ease your burden, Mrs. Stanky?"

"No. I'll be all right. And Laurie will be so happy to know she has an anonymous friend."

CHAPTER 44 – PARTY PLANS
Monday afternoon, December 24, 1945

Boyd drove to pick up his date for the Christmas party. When Johnston had called the day before, Boyd thought long and hard about someone willing to accompany him with short notice. He would have liked to ask Stacy Jo but couldn't quite clear the hurdle of her selling herself at the Gilded Lily. Maybe he'd get to talk to her in the course of the evening and find out the truth of the matter.

Boyd knocked on the door.

"Hello, Boyd. You certainly clean up well. Do I look all right?"

Boyd gave an appraising look at a woman in a dark blue chiffon dress. She had her hair tossed high on her head with a few strands hanging down in a circular, serendipity arrangement. Wearing an antique necklace of pale blue stones it ended with one dangling that held a captured animated star. Boyd noticed that the star moved as he or his date moved. This was a woman who knew how to 'put on the Ritz.'

"You look beautiful."

"Thank you for asking me. I had planned on celebrating by myself. No, actually that's not true. I'd forgotten tonight is Christmas Eve and hadn't planned anything at all."

"It's cold. Do you have a coat?"

"Yes, but it's not very stylish. I've not had occasion to buy anything unpractical."

Boyd helped her with an old brown wool coat. "It'll keep you warm and that's what's important."

On the thirty-minute drive, they talked about the weather, about the runaway boys, about the two bank robberies, and about Santa Claus.

"When I was a little boy I'd get to pick out one present from under the tree to open on Christmas Eve. I always picked out the biggest and heaviest gift I could find. My father picked up on that and sometimes he'd wrap things like a rake or a sack of concrete mix. Next morning I was up at daybreak. With sleep still in the corners of my eyes, I'd run down the hall to see what Santa had delivered in the night. None of his presents were wrapped. These were the things I had been leaving hints about for the previous few months. I played with them for a while then went and rousted my parents out of bed. Minutes later, I had the presents separated and passed around. Usually, there were a couple from my mother to my father and a similar number from my father to my mother, but for me there were dozens. It was a magical time."

"Are your parents still alive?"

"No. Mother died when I was in high school and Dad passed away two years ago."

"Christmas is a sad time of year for those who don't have anyone to share it with."

"I think you're right. But that's not us tonight."

"Will I know anyone at your party, Boyd?"

"One or two. Mayor Bob will be there. You might have seen his picture in the paper. Then there's Harold Greenleaf."

"Harold's going to be there?"

"Yes, ma'am. You know Harold?"

"Indeed I do."

"Stacy, tell me about this party."

"Not much to say. The wives of the city council members have been helping their husbands do projects for the city. They had a list they wanted to get accomplished before Christmas and, now that they've finished, they want to celebrate. I was Boyd's girlfriend and helped a few times so they called me and said it was mandatory I attend."

"But you're going with Lloyd—not Boyd."

"Yes. It might be a little awkward. But Boyd and Lloyd are friends somehow. Lloyd's probably on better terms with Boyd than I am."

"I can't believe you burned his clothes without letting him explain. They might have hauled him to the Gilded Lily on a pretense of going somewhere else. He might be innocent in the entire affair."

"I've wondered about that. Guess I'll find out tonight."

For the next thirty minutes, Stacy Jo used her girlfriend's bedroom to change from a business suit and black pumps to an evening gown and high-heeled shoes. When Lloyd arrived, all he could do was emit a low-level whistle.

Summer Satterfield sat in the middle of her kitchen floor unlacing George's black dress shoes. He'd tramped in the woods behind the school and gotten them muddy along with a good pair of slacks and a heavy gabardine jacket.

"I'm sorry, honey. I was only going to look for a short while. But the longer I was out there, the more important it became. Those boys could freeze in this weather."

"I didn't say anything, Georgie."

Summer took the shoes onto her back porch where she used a kitchen knife to scrape off the mud. She got off what remained by holding the shoes under spewing lukewarm water in her kitchen sink and scrubbing vigorously with a vegetable brush. She dried them with a kitchen towel before smearing black shoe polish from the top of her eyebrows to the tip of her elbows. A little bit of the polish made its way onto the shoes and this she hoped to polish to a glistening luster. She also hoped to wash off the portion that didn't make it to the shoes when she took her shower.

George Satterfield looked at the mess his attractive wife had made and stepped into the shower. After spending most of the day in the woods, he needed a long hot shower to wash away his anxiety.

"George, darling, I need a shower too."

"Come in and join me."

"I would, but it's such a small shower I think it would cramp your style. Besides, I have something special planned for later tonight."

George took his time. Soon he felt the water start to cool and thought, you silly ass. You've used up all the hot water and now the woman who scrubbed your shoes and has half a pound of black shoe polish on her face will have to bathe in cold water. George emerged with wrinkles on his fingers and suggested Summer wait for the heater to warm the water. Summer looked at the clock and decided she didn't have enough time. It was a chilling experience, but she wasn't going to let a little cold water dampen her spirits.

"Damn you, George Satterfield. I might have to take my purse to you once I get out of here."

"Summer, take a navy shower."

"How do you do that?"

"Get wet all over, turn off the water, and soap your entire body. When you've scrubbed yourself clean; turn the water on and rinse off. If you'll step outside, I'll help you get that shoe polish off."

The boys had decided to make a grand entrance at the party planned for the Ritz—not the one in the ballroom but the one in the large conference room. The one where the girls, and the families who had taken them into their homes, would be. The Ritz was going to supply them with a nice meal and presents would be exchanged. They decided this was the proper place and the proper time for them to walk in as heroes with the town's money.

"Spencer, if you could be anything in the world, what would you like to be?"

"I've thought about that. I think I'd like to build bridges and tall buildings. I think that's what engineers do. Architects draw what the engineers build. That also might be an interesting job."

"How about you, Tyrone?"

"I don't know. I don't read as much as the rest of you guys. I don't think I'm smart enough to be an engineer or an architect. Maybe something more along the lines of a farmer or a rancher. I think working the land appeals to me more than being cooped up in an office all day."

"Judd, have you given any thought to what you'd like to be when you grow up?"

"Naw, Terrell. I got a lot of living to do before I have to start making a living. I take that back. I have thought about being a policeman."

"Lawrence?"

"I want to be a college professor. I want to write books and get up in front of the class and talk about how important they are."

"What kind of books?"

"About baseball. And other books about swimming in the Illinois Bayou, canoeing down the Buffalo, exploring caves, hunting for extinct animals. I might like taking people on safaris, although I wouldn't want anyone to shoot the animals with anything other than a camera. I can see myself like Ernest Hemingway, running with bulls, sailing tropical seas, swimming with mermaids."

"Lawrence, you been reading the *National Geographic?*"

"Yep. What about you, Terrell?"

"I think I'd like to be a veterinarian. I've always liked animals. I've thought about hiring on as an assistant. They might need someone to hold a dog while he's getting his shots or to bathe one who's fallen into a slime-covered pond. I've watched a guy insert a hose into a horse's mouth to give him something that kills worms. The horse didn't like that one bit."

"That's everyone but you, Lacy. Is there any particular job you'd like when you grow up?"

"I've considered several, but there's only one for me. I want to help people. I want to restore their faith, to get them back into the fold, and to help them save their souls."

"What job would that be?"

"I'm going to be a priest."

Connie Wiggins gave each girl five dollars and headed to Kress's Five and Dime. They were supposed to make presents to give the boys, but Connie had such a good time teaching the girls the fun involved in housework and cooking that she let the time slip by. Now there wasn't enough time to make something. She'd have to purchase their gifts.

"I've never bought presents for boys. What do you think they'd like?"

Penny said, "Mrs. Wiggins, can I split my money and buy two gifts? I'd like to get something for Terrell just from me."

"Sure, honey. What do you think Terrell would like?"

"Let me think. Have you ever seen anyone play with a paddle ball?"

"A paddle ball?"

"Yes, ma'am. It's a ball attached to a paddle with a rubber band. You pop the ball and it springs away then recoils after reaching the end of the stretch in the rubber band. When the ball comes charging back, you whop it again with the paddle. Some people can keep it going for long periods of time. He might like to have one of those."

"I might like to have one of those," said Laurie. "How about a pocket knife? The boys are always whittling something out of pieces of wood."

"Would Father O'Reilly let them have a knife?"

"Sure. He's the one who taught them how to whittle in the first place."

"How about books?"

"Yeah, some of them are regular customers at the library, especially Lawrence and Spencer. The library lets most people have up to five books at a time, but Lawrence and Spencer have had their limits removed. They can have as many books as they want."

In the Kress's Five and Dime, they bumped into Jesse Bell. "Merry Christmas, Jesse. Girls, this is Mr. Bell. He owns the newspaper."

"We know him. He came to interview us at the orphanage," Laurie extended her hand. "Hello, Mr. Bell."

"Hello, Laurie." Jesse shook Laurie's hand then reached for Penny's. "Thank you both for talking with me." Jesse put his hands in his pockets and rocked back on his heels. "Ladies, are you making some last-minute Christmas purchases?"

"Yes. Some for the girls and I'm letting these two buy presents for the boys. They'll be back soon. They're just staying away long enough for us to regret not giving them any attention. As for me and, I think, for the rest of the town, we've learned our lesson. Are you coming to the party tonight?"

"I am."

Connie and the girls loaded up ten paddle balls and two pocket knives. And Penny had purchased a pair of leather gloves lined with rabbit fur for her older brother. As they left, they waved at Jesse and said they'd see him in a few more hours.

Jesse decided he couldn't go to the party without gifts of his own, so he purchased seven pairs of aviator sunglasses and ten musical boxes in assorted styles.

CHAPTER 45 – THE PARTY OF THE FIRST PART

Monday evening, December 24, 1945

Mayor Bob and his wife, Clarice, were the first ones to arrive. The *maître d'* sat them at one long table down the center of the restaurant and only a few feet from the stage. Faisal Obadiah and Ophelia soon followed. Mayor Bob was into his second drink when Harold Greenleaf and Imogene walked in.

"Did Johnston say he'd talked to Boyd and Stacy Jo?" whispered Mayor Bob to Harold.

Harold leaned toward Bob and said under his breath, "Yeah, Robert. When I talked to Johnston, he'd already spoken with Stacy and said he'd be calling Boyd as soon as he got home. Evidently, Boyd had to make sure someone had their pipes fixed properly."

"Well, he better. Clarice said she had something special planned for after the party and I sure want it to happen. If we don't get Boyd and Stacy Jo back together, my little party after the party might peter out."

At normal volume Mayor Bob said, "Harold, put on this Santa's hat. The women said we all have to wear one so they'll know we're in the spirit."

"Bob, your hat is two sizes too large. It's not supposed to hang down over the ears."

"What's the good of a hat if it doesn't keep your head warm?"

"I don't know. Here's Jerry Millhouse. He looks like he walked off the cover of a fashion magazine. Let's ask him."

Clarice stood up from her chair and walked to greet Mona Millhouse. "How did it go at Ava's today?"

"It was a nightmare. There were more customers than we had places to put them. With my commissions, I made forty-two dollars for Gladys. Betty made fifty Saturday, so all told; we helped Ava at her busiest time and helped Gladys to the tune of almost a hundred dollars. I'm tired but feeling pretty good."

"Have you heard about Harold?"

"No."

"He's promised to dance with Imogene."

"No. That's gotta be worth the price of admission right there."

Summer Satterfield walked over. "Where do I put the presents?"

Clarice said, "Summer, what do you have on your face? And here, on your arm?"

"Shoe polish. Damn stuff won't come off. Georgie almost scraped off my hide trying to remove it. I think he enjoyed the effort."

"Well, I hope it doesn't put a damper on what you have planned for later tonight."

"No chance of that."

"Is that Boyd? Who's the woman on his arm? Where's Stacy Jo?"

"Calm down, Betty. She's probably his mother."

Harold stood at his chair. Boyd dropped two small presents onto the table and said, "Merry Christmas, everyone. Let me introduce Joyce Martin—Stacy Jo's mother."

Boyd introduced Joyce to everyone. When he came to Harold, Joyce said, "I already know this man. Hello, Harry. Merry Christmas."

"J C, you look lovely. I don't think you've aged since I saw you last. Must've been thirty years ago."

"Thank you, Harry. Is this your wife?"

"J C, this is Imogene . . . uh . . . is Stacy Jo your daughter?"

Joyce smiled and nodded as several conversations were going at the same time. After Boyd and Joyce were seated, everyone was now at the party except Stacy Jo and Stone.

George asked Johnston, "Stacy Jo did say she was coming, didn't she?"

"Relax, George. She'll be here."

At that moment Stacy Jo walked in on the arm of Lloyd Garrison.

"Lordy, Lordy, Lordy," said Mayor Bob under his breath. "Looks like we got a storm brewing."

When the couple reached the table, Stacy added two small packages to the pile and introduced Lloyd to everyone. "Mom, what are you doing here?"

"I'm Boyd's date."

"You are?"

"Yes, and who's this young man you have in tow?"

"Mom, you know him. This is Lloyd."

"Pleased to make your acquaintance, Mrs. Martin."

"Nice to meet you, Lloyd."

"Mom, you said Lloyd came to our house to see me. You said he helped you decorate the Christmas tree."

"Not Lloyd dear. It was Boyd." She patted Boyd on the arm.

Stacy Jo sat down wondering how things had gotten so screwed up. Lloyd walked over to Boyd and whispered something in his ear. Boyd pinched his lips and slowly nodded his head. He said, "Thanks, Lloyd, at least you tried."

The waiter walked up and took everyone's order. Stacy Jo ordered a glass of red wine. She planned on switching it later for Lloyd's iced tea. Boyd said he needed a cocktail and settled on a vodka gimlet. Harold ordered a dark beer and most of the women ordered frilly concoctions sporting colorful umbrellas or little monkeys on long stir sticks. Most of these drinks had little alcohol but lots of color.

The band started playing soft orchestral pieces. Occasionally the drummer got carried away with an up-tempo Christmas tune, but for the most part they kept it under control while the restaurant patrons enjoyed sumptuous meals. The band planned on getting livelier a little later when the waiters cleared away the plates.

"Here, Boyd, you got to wear one of these hats. Pass the other one down to Lloyd."

"Hey, Lloyd, were you scared when that guy took the town's money?"

"Out of my pants."

"Why do you think Edwin gave him that warning?"

"I don't know. I don't think Edwin knew him, I just think Edwin wasn't afraid of him like I was."

"Does anyone have an update on Edwin's condition?"

"I was there this afternoon," said Rube Abernathy. "He's still in a deep coma. Gladys said the doctor doesn't holdout much hope he'll ever come out of it."

"Poor Gladys. She really loves Edwin."

"She gave him a shave this morning."

"I don't think she's left his side."

The *maître d'* walked onto the stage and, into the microphone, he announced the name of the band and from what part of the country they called home. He said there had been no new developments in the search for the boys or the man who shot Officer Edwin Stanky. He also said he'd asked the police dispatcher to notify him if anything did come up and that he'd stop the music and make an announcement if they called.

Soon the salads were delivered, more drinks were ordered, and everyone was in high spirits except Stacy Jo and Boyd.

"So, Boyd, what did you want to talk to me about when you came to Skunk Hollow?" Stacy sat three seats to the right of Boyd and on the other side of the table. She had to talk in a loud voice to be heard over the band playing softly, five waiters serving, and seventy-five people eating. Additionally, each table had its own conversation going.

"I wanted to talk to you about—about you burning my clothes. I wanted to forgive you."

"You wanted to forgive me? What about you going to that—that house." Stacy gave her mother a look to see if she comprehended what was being said.

"Oh, that. It was done on a lark. It didn't mean anything. I understand Ophelia has pictures of me holding a stick in one hand and a chair in another. I have all my clothes on—every piece."

"But the intent was still there. And it might not have been the first time you went there."

"Harold, how many times have you been to the Gilded Lily?"

"Just that one time, sugar dumpling."

"Robert?"

"Baby, it was my first time, I swear."

"Jerry?"

"Never. I've never been to that bordello. But, I have heard that they treat you real nice."

"Tell me, Boyd, if you crawled in bed with one of those women would you be fantasizing about me?"

"Stacy Jo, is there a correct answer to that question? May I have a moment to ask the other men how they'd answer a question like that?"

"Damnit, Boyd, I'm talking to you. I'm not in the least bit interested in what the other men fantasized about. So tell me."

"Uh . . . Stacy Jo. Maybe we could talk about this private stuff when we have a little more privacy."

"Stacy Jo. When I was not much older than you, we had a similar problem with a place like the Gilded Lily. People had different attitudes then: more puritanical. Still, some of the women liked having their men go. It took the edge off and allowed them to enjoy their husbands or lovers at a slower and more pleasurable pace. It was a 'wham-bam-thank-you-ma'am' five minutes for those ladies and an hour or longer of delight for us. Your father went on occasion."

Stacy's mouth fell open.

"Have you started working there yet, Stacy Jo?" asked Suzanne.

"Working at the Gilded Lily?" said Stacy Jo.

"Yeah. We understand you heard a woman can make as much as fifty dollars in one night," said Clarice.

"It's not me working there, it's Ophelia."

Several women laughed at the same time.

"She was only pretending to work there so she could steal the pictures and negatives. They were taken by Twinkie of the men while they were naked, fighting the men from Skunk Hollow—all but Boyd. He was still dressed," said Clarice.

Ophelia turned several shades of red. Faisal said, "Honey, you told me you bought those pictures and negatives. But you actually worked there?"

"What pictures?" said Stacy.

"Stacy, you told me you'd seen the pictures and Twinkie was selling them for ten dollars each."

"No, that's what a trip upstairs costs. I don't know anything about pictures. Are you telling me none of you ladies are working at the Gilded Lily? Ophelia said you all worked there."

"Stacy, I don't think that's what I said." Ophelia turned to Faisal, "Honey, I didn't work there. It just looked like I was working."

"Ladies. Please." The *maître d'* stood behind Mayor Bob. "May we have a little decorum over here? You're disrupting the party."

The band had stopped playing, forks had been put down, bodies turned, and heads leaned as the other attendees tried to hear what was being said. They wanted to know more about their mayor and the members of their city council fighting the men from Skunk Hollow while naked and to learn which city council members' wives worked at the Gilded Lily.

From the hallway leading to the conference room and the other party came Stone and his wife, Marge. It was eerie. They saw the center table full of their friends sitting stock still and people from the other tables leaning and looking at the center table. Even the waiters had stopped and were waiting on something. No one said a word or made the slightest noise. Stone and Marge thought about getting a separate table and letting their friends wallow in their own troubles which now seemed to be seeping out to be enjoyed by everyone within earshot.

Clarice stood and motioned for Stone and Marge to join the group.

"What's happening?" asked Marge.

"A little housecleaning," said Clarice.

Boyd started it back up with, "So you're not working at the Gilded Lily?"

"Absolutely not."

Lloyd said, "Will you be working there weekends in the future?"

"You people are crazy. I have never, I am not now, and I do not plan in the future to work at the Gilded Lily—not even if they paid me a hundred dollars a night. Now for two hundred, I might reconsider."

"You're awfully emphatic about that."

Ophelia started laughing. She couldn't stop. She picked up a glass of water, took a big swig and laughed again, spurting out water from the corners of her mouth to the far reaches of the table.

"What were you doing there talking with the brunette?" said Boyd.

"I was looking for you. She's Miss Ryan, my high school English teacher. And Twinkie's my best friend."

"Are you the one who cooked the meal with all the potatoes?"

Stacy Jo looked at her fellow conspirators. No one gave her a frown so she asked, "Did your house burn down?"

"No."

"Then, yes, I did."

"For what purpose? To show me you could cook potatoes after saying for months you couldn't?"

"No. To ask you to forgive me for being so difficult when I thought you didn't love me."

"I'll take that into consideration."

Johnston kicked Boyd under the table. Leaning forward with one hand to the side of his mouth, he whispered, "Buster, you're playing with the sex life of every man here."

Boyd looked around the table. Every man was looking at him and every woman was looking at Stacy Jo. "Stacy, I think we can work this out." Boyd reached into his pocket and pulled out a small box wrapped in red paper and tied in a purple bow. "I have a Christmas present for you and I think now is the right time for you to open it."

People from around the room applauded. They thought Boyd had extricated himself quite nicely from a sticky situation. Even two band members clapped.

Boyd passed the gift down the table with Suzanne handing it across the table to Stacy Jo. Stacy had tears in her eyes as she grabbed for the gift. With the practiced talent some women have of tearing open a package with the greatest of ease and in a minimum period of time, Stacy looked down at a jewelry box. She stopped. Did she want to open this? What if it was earrings? She hesitated, closed her eyes, and lifted the top. From her left came the sound she'd hoped for—envy. A drawn out "Ohhh" dipping in pitch on the end. It was the sound of envy and when she heard it, she opened her eyes to see the largest diamond on a wedding ring she'd ever seen.

"Is it real?"

"It is." A pause. "Stacy Jo, will you marry me?"

Stacy Jo had the ring out of the box and onto her finger. "Boyd, I'll take your request into consideration."

Some people laughed, some clapped, and others cried. Stacy Jo kissed Faisal and told him to pass it around. Faisal turned to Ophelia. "Honey, I love you. But we need to talk about your new job." He kissed his wife of fifteen years. She turned and kissed Johnston Baker who thought this was the best proposal he'd ever been a party to. He kissed Betty, who kissed Rube, and on it went. When Joyce kissed Boyd, Stacy Jo jumped up from her chair and ran around the table and plopped down in Boyd's lap. She put her arms around him while he was trying his best to kiss Clarice sitting to his left.

When the kiss had made it all the way around the table, Lloyd turned to an empty chair. Clarice stood up and said. "Let me be the first to propose a toast to the newest full-fledged member of our troupe.

Here's to you, Stacy, and to your union with Boyd, the bravest man here."

Glasses rose, chinked, and their contents guzzled.

Clarice continued, "Are any of these gifts unsuitable for a child?"

Each person thought and each person shook his or her head from side to side.

"Then let's take a break and march them down the hall to where the orphans are being entertained. Let's give them the gifts."

The waiter arrived with the first of the entrees. He winked, did an about-face, and headed back to the kitchen. The entire room echoed with coordinated clapping. The entourage from the long center table grabbed their presents. They ended up holding the presents in their left hands and the shoulder of the person in front with their right hand. In this fashion, wearing tilted Santa's hats, they danced out of the restaurant in a line like drunken revelers in a Mardi Gras parade. They stepped to the beat of jazz by the band and the continued clapping of the audience.

CHAPTER 46 – THE PARTY OF THE SECOND PART

Monday evening, December 24, 1945

The boys spent the morning calculating the right time to leave to have their arrival create the greatest impact. Because it got dark so early and the party was supposed to start at seven, they decided to leave for their return an hour before dark. After the lunch of warmed-up breast of turkey and cranberry salad, they tidied up the hideout. The boys stuffed their clothes in pillowcases, burned their trash with the last of the wood they had accumulated, and put the jar of sauerkraut in the wagon. The other food items they placed on rocks for the scavenging of the animals.

As the sun started to descend over the horizon, Terrell sat Lacy in the Red Flyer wagon next to the brown leather satchel and the sauerkraut. They headed to town.

Before reaching the city limit, a car approached and stopped in the middle of the highway. Two men got out, hugged the boys, slapped each other on the back, and with their arms interlinked, danced a circle in the street first in one direction and then in the other. The two men were so overcome with jollity that they stumbled over a boy's stuffed pillowcase and landed on their backsides. The boys laughed, the two men laughed, and two black crows in a nearby tree laughed. The men sat up and asked if they could give the boys a lift into town. The two men said they were mighty proud that the boys had been able to weather the harsh conditions and they had a thousand questions. The boys said no, they wanted to come back the same way they left. So with the boys in the lead, the two men escorted them by driving down the middle of the road and honking their horn. Other cars joined in. They soon had a parade formed. It was a loud cacophony of merriment as they passed through the residential area and into the business section of town.

When the train of boys and cars reached Main Street, people started magically appearing. They had come out of houses, barns, riding stables, businesses, and parked cars to walk beside the boys.

Someone noticed the brown satchel and let out a wonderful cowboy yelp that somehow ended in a yodel. More and more people realized the boys had the town's money. Soon everyone knew as word passed from one reveler to another. On the steps of the Ritz Grand Hotel and Ballroom, Terrell picked up Lacy and Spencer picked up the satchel. They marched like a disciplined army squad into the building. People in the restaurant heard the commotion outside their door and thought the people from the center table were now having a free-for-all in the foyer. They left their tables to place wagers on whether the men or the women would prevail.

The boys plowed on and stepped through the door to the conference room.

Earlier that evening Connie Wiggins and other Dancing Deer citizens had arrived at a conference room decorated by the hotel staff with a Christmas tree and lighted ropes. The tree was drenched in ferns, holly, pine cones, and ornaments. Ornaments also hung from the ceiling and a big net held hundreds of balloons suspended high overhead. Games were set up, a large table held every kind of dessert imaginable, and a corner of the room was cordoned off holding presents stacked waist-high. The entire town had contributed.

Father O'Reilly and two nuns mingled with the families as Jesse and a photographer took pictures for the paper. Jesse's assistant Mitzi followed her boss's every step, getting names, opinions, and statements.

At seven, Father O'Reilly took the microphone and thanked everyone for coming. Besides the families lodging the girls and Andy, other families and stray children just wanted to be there. They came from Skunk Hollow, Possum Point, and Cakebread. One family came all the way from Moccasin Gap. The large conference room held big conventions and it looked like this one had been put on by Santa Claus himself.

"Ladies, gentlemen, boys, and girls, thank you all for coming to this little get-together. Before we start a delightful evening of fun and frivolity, let me give thanks to our Lord. Please bow your heads." He waited a moment for all to become silent, and then said, "Dear Heavenly Father. It is You, we honor and obey. It is to You, glory and homage we pay. Please, Father, watch out for our six lost boys. Keep them from harm's way and restore Edwin Stanky's health. Be with each family as we honor the birth of your Son and our Savior. It's in Jesus' name we pray. Amen."

Several other people added their own amens.

"Please find a seat. The waiters are here with the food. As they wheel the cart from one table to the next, give them your choices. The items available are written on the tent cards placed in the middle of the tables. Mr. Potter said for each to eat as much as he or she possibly could, and if you order more than you can eat you'll have to do the dishes. No, he didn't say that. What he said was to give them whatever they want and as much as they'll take. But I want everyone to know the dessert table overflows and you'll want to save room for some of that. There's soda pop, apple juice, lemonade, milk, and cool, clear water to drink. Eggnog will be served with the desserts. Thank you all again for coming. Now let's have some fun."

When they had finished the meal and demolished the dessert table, Jesse stood on a wooden box and suggested all the children come forward. "There are so many presents each child here—everyone who thinks he might have been included on Santa's list whether orphan or not—will be able to participate. Since the presents are wrapped without any indication as to the age bracket, if you receive a present meant for someone younger or older than yourself or if you're a girl opening a present for a boy or vice versa, place the present on this long empty table and you'll be handed another. When it's your turn, you may have anything on the table or get one not yet opened. But before we start handing out the gifts we have some very special gifts from the orphan girls to the orphan boys. Andy will accept for his lost brothers. So if the orphans will come forward and bring their gifts."

Ten little girls came forward and put their presents on the table where Andy sat.

"All right, Father O'Reilly, if you would have the waiters bring in the table the boys left for the girls."

Father Donovan O'Reilly directed the efforts of four waiters as they brought in two tables containing the doll-house furniture the boys had whittled from small blocks of scrap wood. The furniture was separated into ten piles with a name scribbled on a piece of paper taped to the table in front of each pile. As the girls ran forward, the conference room door burst open.

Terrell entered carrying Lacy, followed by Lawrence, Tyrone, and Judd. Spencer was the last one and he carried the bank bag with the town's money. The town's residents were on the boys like jam on a biscuit. In a mass confusion, everyone wanted to touch the boys to make sure they were okay. When the clamor abated, Spencer found Chief of Police, Steve Trent, who sat close by with his wife and fourteen-year-old daughter, Polly. Spencer handed the satchel to Officer Trent and said the robber asked them to return the money he stole.

The first two men to find the boys on the highway said they had been looking for them non-stop since Saturday morning. Their wives were doubly happy for the boys' rescue.

Johnston Baker bent down to Lacy and said, "Were you the supervisor for the operation, Lacy?"

"Yes, sir, but I let Terrell think he was in charge just the same."

Jesse asked his photographer if he'd taken any pictures and received an enthusiastic, "Yes, dozens."

Jesse asked Terrell to the microphone to tell the crowd how they'd spent the last few days and where they had sheltered.

"Well, sir, we were in God's hands. When we needed food we found it. When we needed water, he provided that as well. When the snow started coming down so you couldn't see your hand in front of your face, we stumbled onto an abandoned farm building. When we realized the windows were broken, he provided feed sacks for us to plug them with and when we needed a fire, he provided the knowledge to make that happen as well. We placed our faith where it would do us the most good. God says for us to challenge him and we did."

"Were you aware the city had every citizen scouring the town and the countryside looking for you?"

"No, sir. We were headed to California when the storm derailed us. Then the man gave us the briefcase and told us to take it back. We knew then that we'd have to postpone our adventure. California was too far away. We're now going to rest up and head to Florida where the P.T. Barnum and Bailey Circus spends the winter."

"Tell us about the man who robbed the bank."

"He never said his name. I think he had an awakening after listening to Lacy. Last night he left after everyone was asleep. This morning we found the briefcase and a note saying he was sorry for shooting Mr. Stanky. He said he'd take back the bullet if he could. He also took the blame for the Skunk Hollow bank robbery, saying that the man named Lenny was only doing what he had told him to do. That Lenny didn't know he was robbing a bank. Spencer, give the note to Officer Trent."

Jesse looked out over the audience. "Are there any questions any of you would like to ask the boys?"

Several hands shot up. "Okay, step to the microphone one at a time."

A man stepped forward and said, "Young man, what made you and the others decide to leave?"

"We felt like we were the protectors for the girls and when they didn't need our protection anymore, our job was done. It was time to get on with our lives. We headed to California where prosperity awaits any person not afraid of a little hard work."

Officer Steve Trent's daughter, Polly, stepped up and said, "Terrell, is there any way we can ask for a second chance?"

Terrell said, "I'd like to give that some thought before I answer. And I can't personally speak for everyone as each of us has our own road to travel. Get back with me in a couple of days. Your name is Polly, isn't it?"

"Yes."

Jesse took the microphone and said, "All right. Let's hold the rest of the questions until the boys have had something to eat. I don't suppose you ate manna on your way back?"

"No, but we did have a nice lunch," said Terrell

"Make way. Give the boys a seat." Jesse waited a moment while several people stood up offering their chair. "If you boys will tell the waiters what you'd like, they'll get it for you." Jesse set the microphone back in its holder and turned to his assistant. "Mitzi, did you get all of that?"

"Yes, sir. Every word."

CHAPTER 47 – BOTH PARTIES IN FULL SWING
Monday evening, December 24, 1945

Back in the bistro things were getting back to normal. The band had followed the patrons without knowing what had happened. Also, they preferred not to play to an empty house. They were the first ones back so when the remaining diners returned it was to Christmas songs and other up-beat compositions.

Walking back into the restaurant Mona Millhouse said to her husband Jerry, "That was exciting. When those boys burst in it was sheer pandemonium. Santa Claus flying through the door on an airborne sleigh would not have made a more joyful impact."

At the table, Stacy Jo traded places with her mother and wouldn't let Boyd out of her sight. She would have gone with him into the men's room had she not been stopped by Johnston. "Honey, he's not going to slip away. I'll see to it that he makes it back to the table."

"I'm sorry, I wasn't paying attention. Like a lemming I was following at his heel wherever he went."

"Go back to the table and start planning with your mother."

"Good Lord, I've got to set a date." Stacy turned on her heel and returned to the table a little red-faced.

"Mom, it was Boyd who was waiting for me and ended up sleeping on the divan?"

"Yes, dear."

"And it was Boyd who helped you decorate the Christmas tree?"

"Yes, dear."

"And it was Boyd who made all those telephone calls—one with an urgent message?"

"No, dear. That was either Lloyd, Gerald, or Patrick."

"Mom, who's Gerald and Patrick?"

"I was hoping you would tell me, dear."

Clarice asked, "When are you planning the wedding?"

Suzanne said, "Let me see that ring."

"Stacy, I'm so glad you and Boyd are getting married. We were worried about him getting that disease the men in Skunk Hollow are getting. You know—vomiting blood and the boils."

"No, I don't know."

Lloyd said, "I've heard about it. Boyd told Edwin and me Thursday. It was hideous the way he described the way those boils burst open and stained the skin. Made me shudder. I'll never go to the Gilded Lily now that you're not going to be working there."

"Lloyd, were you planning on visiting me at the Gilded Lily?"

"Uh . . . just to . . . just to make sure you were okay." Lloyd turned to talk to Mona Millhouse on his right but Mona's eyes were big and her lips pinched shut. Lloyd looked back to Stacy and noticed every woman was looking at him with piercing stares.

"And those questions you had about what the procedures were and what the probable charges would be was only an innocent interest in my welfare."

"Stacy Jo, every one of us thought you were going to start work at the Gilded Lily," said Clarice. "We thought you needed more money to make up for the loss in pay from the bank in Skunk Hollow."

"Hey, babe, want to order a dessert?" Boyd had returned, pulling out his chair.

"Not now. I have to keep my weight down in case I have to work at the Gilded Lily."

Boyd looked around the table. The men thought it prudent to keep their mouths shut, and the women waited to hear what remark Boyd would make.

"How do you like the ring, honey?" Boyd took a drink of water.

"Boyd, tell us about the men in Skunk Hollow vomiting blood and breaking out in boils."

"Damn." He paused a moment then finished with, "Stacy, would you like to dance?"

"Yes, I would, but you'll eventually have to answer my questions."

Boyd got up from his seat and took Stacy Jo's hand. "How many questions you got?"

"Just the one right now."

"Okay, I'll answer all your questions if you'll answer all mine."

Stacy Jo put her left hand around Boyd's neck as they reached the dance floor. "Sounds fair to me. What questions do you have?"

"I want to know about the banana thing, for one."

"Uh . . . Boyd, how about a compromise? No more questions. We'll have a new beginning. You and me, no baggage."

"I'll agree to that."

Stacy Jo stopped dancing. She put both hands to the sides of Boyd's face, as if centering a target, and kissed him passionately.

"He must have given her the correct answer," said Clarice.

After the boys finished eating—with everyone watching their every bite—Jesse suggested the orphan boys open their presents from the girls, which turned out to be three pocket knives, two compasses, one pair of binoculars, and one wrist watch.

Jesse asked Mitzi to bring over two large bags and one small one. "These are from the paper." He handed Terrell the small bag and Penny and Laurie the two large bags. "Go ahead, they're the same."

Terrell handed each boy, including Andy, a pair of aviator sunglasses. Penny and Laurie handed out music boxes. Each girl had to wind the spring and play the melody right then. It was instantaneous cacophony as there were several different tunes and, even when the tunes were the same, they were unsynchronized.

Marge, Stone, and their three children brought out two tables from the next room that contained doll houses, yo-yos, and tops. "These are courtesy of the Dancing Deer City Council and the Mayor. They're handmade."

The orphans were not used to getting more than one or two gifts and something like a bible from the church, so they were overwhelmed. Lacy said, "These are all well and good and I, for one, am certainly going to enjoy playing with what I've been given. But I think we all need to reflect on the reason for the season. Three wise men gave gifts to the infant Jesus and we as Christians have continued that tradition by giving each other presents. We don't have presents to give in return— just those pieces of doll-house furniture. Certainly nothing like what we are being given."

Jesse picked up the microphone and spoke for everyone there. "Your safe return to Dancing Deer was all we wanted."

CHAPTER 48 – EDWIN
Tuesday morning, December 25, 1945

Gladys left Edwin for only brief periods of time. Last night, Christmas Eve, for example, she left to attend the party for the orphans. She had a good time, especially when the boys charged through the door carrying the town's money. What a charge they delivered. Electricity flooded the room when they arrived. The ones most happy, though, were the girls. Their eyes lit up like Christmas trees.

It was a wonderful time, and then she talked with Connie Wiggins about Laurie.

"Edwin, I've brought someone for you to meet. Edwin, this is Laurie. Here, take his hand, Laurie. She's the one who wrote the letter to you. You remember, I read it to you yesterday."

A nurse was standing in the doorway, "Gladys, Doctor Rayne was here on his rounds early this morning. He told me to call when you got here. I'm afraid he's got bad news."

"Edwin isn't responding, is he?"

"No, Gladys, he's not."

"Laurie, you stay here while I talk with the nurse."

Gladys nodded to the hall. Then she and the nurse walked into the waiting room next door. "What can you tell me?"

"Gladys, I don't know anything. The doctor doesn't confide his feelings to anyone other than the patients or their families. I just know that he's not happy with Edwin's chart and that he wants to talk with you this morning."

"Has he tried everything available?"

"Yes, ma'am, but you better let him tell you that. I'm not supposed to say anything."

"Okay, you go call him. Laurie and I are here for the rest of the day." Gladys slowly walked into Edwin's room, her head hung low. The weight of the world pushed down on her shoulders.

"Laurie, it might soon be just the two of us." Tears streamed down her cheeks. She slumped into the chair she'd been sleeping in and wiped away the tears with the palm of one hand.

It took Gladys a few minutes to talk without choking. "Laurie, this tube is dripping a saline substance into his system so he doesn't dehydrate, and this one drains away his urine. This machine measures his heartbeat and these two graphs plot his blood pressure. The top one measures systolic pressure. That's the pressure when his heart's pumping. The bottom one measures the diastolic pressure. That's the pressure when his heart's at rest, or between beats. Between these gray lines is normal. When the pen graphs above the top gray line he has high blood pressure. That is symptomatic of hypertension. It can also lead to a stroke or an aneurysm. When the line goes below the bottom gray line, he has low blood pressure. See how low Edwin's line is? It's well below what's normal.

"This machine pumps oxygen into his lungs. They had to hook it up because he was getting too weak to breathe on his own. You still want to be a nurse?"

"No, Mrs. Stanky, I want to be a doctor."

"You take out your needlepoint and entertain yourself. I want to sit beside my husband. After the doctor comes by, I'll take you to Mr. and Mrs. Wiggins' house. They've invited us for the Christmas meal. Then you'll stay the night with them while I come back here to be with Edwin. Is that all right with you?"

"Yes, ma'am, but I'd rather come back with you."

"We'll see."

Laurie went to the big chair and pulled out the needlepoint Gladys had given her. She artistically pushed the colored thread through the material according to the pattern. Gladys pulled up a folding chair next to Edwin's bed and held his hand in hers.

"Dear Lord, Edwin needs your help. We know you can do all things, so please heal his body. Edwin is a wonderful man. I'm not asking for me, though you know how much I need him. I'm asking for everyone. Edwin is such a loving and compassionate man that when he goes everyone will suffer a loss. If it be your will that Edwin leave us to be with you, then I know Edwin will understand. I won't, but he will. He's stronger than me. If I could give my life to save his I would.

Please, Lord." Gladys wiped the tears from her eyes. "I ask this in Jesus' precious name. Amen."

"Edwin, do you remember the first time we met? My parents had just moved to Dancing Deer from Georgia and enrolled me in the elementary school. I didn't know anyone and was scared. At recess, you asked if you could show me around. You showed me which swings worked, which ones swung crooked, and which ones would put splinters in a person's backside. I learned from you how the teachers announced recess was over, where the ropes and hopscotch bean bags were kept, and where I could get a drink of water. I thought you were the most wonderful person in the whole world. I still do." She stood, leaned over, and kissed his forehead. "Edwin, I love you."

"All through fourth, fifth, and sixth grades I kept up with you. Soon I realized it wasn't me you were trying to impress. You did the same thing to every new student. It was a job you'd assumed: make the new students feel at home, let them know they had a friend, answer their questions, and remove their anxiety. I wasn't the only girl who loved you. Everyone you were nice to thought you were the one for her.

"In the seventh grade I started scheming to get you to ask me to the Valentine's Day Dance. I planned an elaborate ruse and then saw it crumble when you asked Mary Lou Jenkins. I was so distraught; I decided if I couldn't go with you, I wouldn't go at all.

"In the eighth grade I put on some weight and was too embarrassed to ask anyone to anything. You came over and sat beside me in the cafeteria. You asked me how my day was going and if I needed any help with math. I was awestruck. I couldn't get a word out, I just nodded. After school, we sat under an apple tree while you showed me how to do algebra.

"In the ninth grade you and your family moved away and I was broken-hearted. Then one day, I received a letter from you. It was the most wonderful day of my life. I paraded around the house holding the paper up for everyone to see. I spent the next two days writing my reply, tearing it up, and re-writing. When it came time to mail the perfect final version, I had lost your envelope and didn't have an address. That was the worst day of my life. I made my dad take me to the city dump, but it was no use. We couldn't find it.

211

In the eleventh grade, you wrote again. This time I wrote down your address before I even opened the letter. You sent a picture. I still carry that picture everywhere I go. It's a little ragged now but more precious to me than any other thing I own, except for my wedding ring. Two weeks later was the Valentine's Day Dance and a rather handsome young man asked me to go with him. I accepted and imagined he was you for the entire evening. He never asked me out again. In the twelfth grade, I wrote and asked if you would take me to my senior prom. Honey, do you remember that night? I didn't want it to end. You picked me up in your dad's car. I had the most marvelous time. When you brought me back home at midnight and kissed me on my doorstep, you remember what I said? I said, 'I will.' You said, 'Will what?' and I said, 'Marry you.' We got married that summer."

"Hello, Gladys. I'm glad you came to see Edwin, even though it's Christmas Day. I was planning on calling if you didn't. Have a seat, Gladys, we need to talk."

"Doctor, can't you make him well? I can't live without Eddy."

"I'm sorry, Gladys, his blood pressure started a slow decline last night. I gave him every medicine available, but nothing worked. We tried our best."

Doctor Rayne took Gladys' hand. "Gladys, his body is shutting down."

He walked to Edwin's bedside. "See this graph." The doctor pointed to the bottom of the two graphs. "Uh . . . Gladys . . . uh, his blood pressure is . . ." Doctor Rayne went around the bed and thumped the blood pressure monitor with his index finger. "Well, I'll be. Are you some sort of miracle worker, Gladys? When we decided none of the drugs were working I had the nurse take him off the medications completely. She called me a half hour ago saying it was so low he was barely alive. Now his blood pressure is the highest it's been since they first wheeled him into my surgery room. What did you do?"

"I prayed and I told him I loved him." Gladys was weeping openly as she grabbed Edwin's hand and squeezed hard enough to make his fingers go white.

"Careful, girl. You don't want to lose him now, not after bringing him back this far. I had given up hope. Maybe there is a healing power in prayer and a woman's love."

"And God's love."

"Yes, His too."

The End

Author Bio

Ron Lambert, an Examined Life

As an accountant in a small West Texas town, I spend my days studying the bank statements and tax returns of other people's businesses. I classify, summarize, and display their financial transactions in some meaningful format. I love creating order out of chaos.

I'm middle-aged and twice married—with the second blessed from heaven. Four grown children, their children, two bobbing tails of barking energy, and one sly cat round out my cache of treasure.

Over the years, I have owned and operated two boutique retail stores, several service businesses, one ranch, and one restaurant. I have been prosperous and poor, with wild fluctuations in between. At present, being neither rich nor destitute, I consider my status as deeply entrenched in middle-class—a term bandied about by politicians and economists.

In an effort to restore my youth, I purchased an old sofa on two wheels. Since that initial existential groping, I have occasionally strapped sacks of clothes, maps, and a compass that doesn't seem to work onto the back cushion. After kissing my wife, I set out for adventure and story. Usually, after only a week or so, I realize what I left behind was more important than what I set out to find and drive a day and a night hell-bent-for-leather back home.

I then settle into an old and comfortable routine. I read a few books, attend a few plays, daydream of new horizons, and plan my next adventure. I kept a journal on my first excursion. It was such an exhilarating experience: rewriting the journal and incorporating the pictures I took that I became intoxicated to the point I wrote a novel.

At present, with pen on fire, I have just finished my eighth book—actually traveling in untested waters by writing a book for young adults.

I'll win prestigious awards and be asked to speak at the local library if someone would read what I have written.

If you're looking for an evening spent with colorful and mesmerizing characters, if you want to immerse yourself in a rollicking good story, enthrall yourself to the point of madness, go two days without bathing, then have I got a story for you.

Additional Novels

The Dancing Deer Story

All books are available as Trade Paperbacks in perfect binding at www.printersguildpublishing.com and from several fine retailers in Columbus and Weimar, Texas.

Dancing Deer (Book 1)

Dancing Deer is the embodiment of small-town America. When asked, she sent her sons to war. This is the story of The Calhoun—one of those boys. It's also about his fellow combatants, the men he served, the men he fought, and the women he loved.

There is the French Resistance, the German Gestapo, Midge at the Mike, Anzio Annie, the Gustav Line, and the US Army's Forty-Fifth Infantry campaigning from Sicily through Italy, France, and Germany to push back the formidable Germans. But this story is so much more.

Find a comfortable chair and settle in with a great new book. You won't be disappointed.

The Last Dance (Book 2)

Bill Potter is charged with murdering his Friday night squeeze. His bumbling lawyer steps out of a dead-end job of contracts and leases to save Bill from being strapped to "Old Spanky." Bill's wife returns after a twenty-year absence to muddy the waters and it's up to her and Pepe, the womanizing Resistance fighter and WWI spy from France, to solve the case.

The Measure of a Man (Book 3)

A group of Cuban immigrants decide to barnstorm the Midwest, entertaining the towns they come to with a game of ball. When they get to Dancing Deer the men on the city council con Bill Potter into a wager for more than they could afford to lose. Bill's position is that the Men from Dancing Deer will prevail. With a team of misfits and one win under their belts, Bill goes searching for a new manager. His ex-wife is traveling throughout the Western US with Pepe, the French womanizer. She knows more about ball than anyone and he has to convince her to come back and once again save him from the wolves at the door.

Lost in Appalachia (Book 4)

The head of Dancing Deer's Police Department is lost in the mountains of West Virginia. Suffering from an injury, he can't remember who he is or why he's lost. Two kids take him in and hide him from a determined fiancée. The chief of police is in the process of teaching the kids how to read when the fiancée posts a big reward for knowledge of his whereabouts. The chief thinks he must have committed a major crime for someone to pony up such a large bounty.

While the chief awaits the inevitable and worries about what kind of person he really is and what crimes he's committed, the children take measures into their own hands. Their rationale is there will be no one to teach them to read if their new friend is carted off to jail.

Christmas in Dancing Deer (Book 5)

St. Bartholomew's Orphanage is being consolidated, but the children don't want to be separated. They're working on an alternative plan to present to the church when the women of Dancing Deer decide to bring the orphan girls into their homes for the holidays. Left, and by themselves, the orphan boys leave in the snow three days before Christmas.

While the good citizens of Dancing Deer search for the boys a desperate man robs their bank and speeds out of town. He is fast approaching a pivotal moment in his life—a chance encounter where evil comes face to face with good.

Beggarman, Thief (Book 6)

The story of a bank robber who finds his moment of epiphany in a shack with six lost little boys. He goes home after twenty years on the lamb to have Christmas with his family and to right his wrongs. But he finds his past is in hot pursuit and the new life he has found is in jeopardy. He runs away in the clutches of a pretty lady evangelist who is taking her show on the road to the very town where he committed his last crime.

Toe to Toe with A Drunken Philosopher (Book 7)

This is really one story in three parts. First we have the high school philosophy teacher who has to resign his position much as Aristotle had to when the authorities in Athens came looking for him. Part number two is of an indigent Irish family who emigrates from the Emerald Isle. The little Irish boy in the family grows up to become a priest. The third part pits the philosopher and the priest in a contest of wits.

Racing the Wind (Book 8, Written for young adults)

The story of a boy with plans someday to build bridges or design skyscrapers. He decides to pay for his education by building a racer and winning the Soapbox Derby. Problems, orchestrated by his main adversary, creep into the racer's production. The boy has to rely on the help of a fellow classmate—a girl—to find the source of his problem and to finish the racer and the race.

For All the Marbles (Book 9, Written for children but just now seeping into my consciousness)

Eston's best friend, Ben, is a little older, a little bigger, and a lot slower. The other kids have always taken advantage of Ben. Now a bully has won all of Ben's marbles. Eston promised he'd win them back but ended up losing his as well. This is the story of how Eston takes a dangerous new course of action: one that will cleanse the schoolyard of bullying and win back the lost loot.